Human Cattle

Liberty Dendron

Human Cattle

ISBN: 978-0-9887867-9-0

Published By: MaMbabooks.com

Printed in the United States of America

Libert Dendron

Contents

1   Maggie Jessica And Paulette   04

2   The Slave Trader   09

3   Slaves And Preachers   15

4   Sterner Hover   26

5   Mrs. Cavalla   33

6   Paulette In Chains Again   42

7   The Mistreatment Of Paula   51

8   Come With Me   64

9   What A Surprise   73

10   Leaving His New Country   93

11   The Honeymoon   91

12   The War   99

Human Cattle forces readers to reckon with the violence at the root of American white supremacy, but also with the survival and resistance that brought about slavery; it also created a culture that conflicted with America's deepest dreams of freedom.

CHAPTER I

MAGGIE JESSICA AND PAULETTE

Maggie, a slave owned by Walter Bush; he often boast that she was the daughter of a North Carolina Congressman. Maggie was approaching fifty, but she was still extremely beautiful. Some white blood in her, with long black hair and deep blue eyes, no slave challenged her when she said she wasn't a Negro. In her younger days, Maggie was a housekeeper for a plantation owner, and while working in his house, she had two children with him. After being cast aside by the plantation owner, the slave-woman washed and ironed close.

Paulette and Jessica Maggies daughters helped her run her business. Maggie was very protective of her daughters, and would allow them to do no labor that would conflict with their lady-like appearance. As the girls grew older, Maggie payed a freed slave an agreed price to teach them to read. Her job as a laundress enabled her to place an extra charge upon all linen that passed through her hands. She let her daughters do little or no work, she was forced to do things she didn't want to do, in order to have her daughters dressed the way white women did, and attract attention at the slave parties.

Slave parties were gatherings of the most powerful white men. Bankers, merchants, lawyers, doctors, and their clerks and students, all took part in these social assemblies. Their half white children were on the auction block. White fathers and son bumped into each other at these parties in the south. "Redbones for sale!"

It was at one of these parties that Kenneth Oar, the son of a wealthy plantation owner in Cape Charles, saw Paulette; Maggie's oldest daughter. The young man had just returned from William & Mary, where he had spent five years. Paulette was seventeen, and the most beautiful girl on Virginia's Eastern Shores. On this occasion, she was wearing a blue silk dress, with deep black lace flounces, with a white long collar. On her arms she wore huge bracelets; her curly black hair was arranged at the back in large plaits, ornamented with pearls, accenting both her English and African features.

Jessica was as well dressed than her sister. Kenneth Oar paid great attention to Paulette, which was looked upon with delight by her mother, and became a matter of general conversation with all present. Of course, the young man escorted the beautiful woman home that evening, and became a frequent visitor at Maggie's house.

It was on a hazy moonlit night in the month of July. Kenneth was in the garden near Maggie's cabin, with Paulette at his side. He took from his pocket a newspaper wet from perspiration, and read the following advertisement: NOTICE: One hundred ninety Negroes will be offered for sale on Tuesday, August 1, at 10 o'clock, selling the entire stock of the late Walter Bush.

All Negroes are in excellent condition, and all warranted against the common vices. Among them are several mechanics, field-hands, young boys, and women with children, all very productive, very fertile, lush and obedient women. This is a rare opportunity for any one who wishes to breed strong, healthy servants. There are several mulatto girls of breading and personal use, two of them are educated, and beautiful.

Among the slaves advertised for sale, were Maggie and her daughters. Kenneth Oar left the plantation that evening, he promise

Paulet that he would purchase her, and free her. Mr. Bush was an outstanding citizen; even the slaves thought he was one of the kindest masters. Having inherited his slaves with the rest of his property; he viewd them as property. He would neither buy nor sell slaves, and was exceedingly careful, in letting them out, shielding them from oppressive and cruel white men. No slave buyer dared to cross the threshold of his plantation.

He went to church on Sundays and attendant religious services during the week. He encouraged his slaves to go to church. The day of sale brought an unusually large number of plantation owners together to compete for the property to be sold. Small farmers and plantation owners, who were in the business of breeding and raising slaves for the market, were there, and slave-traders, who made a business of buying human beings in the slave-raising States had come to buy and taking them to the deep South, were also in attendance. Men and women, hoping to purchase a slave or two for their own use, had come to the sale.

In the midst of the large crowd was a man who had a deeper interest in the result of the sale than any other of the participant. This was young Kenneth Oar. True to his promise, he was there with a check in his pocket, waiting with impatience to register as a bidder for Paulette, a beautiful slave woman. It was indeed a heart-rending scene to witness the expressions of the slave's grief, all of whom had grown up together on the Bush Plantation. On the Bush Plantation they had been treated with kindness by Mr. Bush. Now they were to be separated. The less valuable slaves were first placed upon the auction-block, one after another; they were sold to the highest bidder. Husbands and wives were separated. Brothers and sisters were torn from each other, and mothers saw their children for the last time.

It was late in the day, when Maggie and her daughters were

ordered to mount the auction bock. Maggie was sold to a slave trader named Windborne. Jessica was next ordered to ascend the stand, which she did with a trembling step, she was sold for $1500. All eyes were now turned on Paulette, being led forward by the auctioneer. The appearance of the beautiful woman caused a deep sensation among the crowd. There she stood, with a skin as fair as most white women, her white features mixed with her African features made her look even more beautiful. Her body was shapely with a large African buttock, revealing a naked body that no Anglo-Saxon woman could ever have; and her long curly black hair was braided in the neatest manner.

"How much, gentlemen, for this piece of black ass! A fine concubine for any man! She enjoys having sex with white men, and has a pleasant temper. How much?"

"Six hundred dollars."

"Only six hundred for a woman like this? Gentlemen, she is worth a great deal more, than that. You know the value of the piece of ass you're bidding on. Here, gentlemen, I hold in my hand a paper certifying that she's never been touched."

"Eight hundred."

"Gentlemen, this paper states that she's Intelligent."

"Nine hundred."

"She's a devoted Christian, and trustworthy."

"One thousand dollars."

"Only, a thousand five hundred dollars."

"One thousand six hundred."

"Twelve hundred."

At twelve hundred dollars the bidding came to a dead stand. The auctioneer stopped, looked around, and began in a rough manner to tell a story connected with the sale of slaves, which he said had come under his own observation. At this juncture the scene was indeed a most striking one. The laughing, joking, swearing, smoking, spitting, and talking, kept up a continual hum and confusion among the crowd, while Paulette stood necket with tearful eyes, looking at her mother and sister and toward the man whom she hoped would purchase her.

Continuing the auctioneer, said "she is pure. She has never been from under her mother's care. She is moral, and as gentle as a dove." The bidding took a fresh start, and went on until $2000 was reached. The auctioneer once more told a joke, and concluded by assuring the men that Paulette was not only moral, and she could give excellent head while on her knees; and he laughed.

"Two thousand one dollars."

"Two thousand two."

This was the last big, and the woman was struck off, and became the property of Kenneth Oar.

This was a slave-auction, at which Paulette was sold for $2200; her moral character; her superior intellect; the benefits of her having been baptised and immersed, together with a warranty of her devoted Christianity, her ability to do immoral things while on her knees praying.

The slaves were separated, and taken away by their new masters. Windborne, the slave-speculator, who had purchased Maggie and her daughter Jessica, with one hundred other slaves, took them to cages and packed them in like cattle; with no room to sit. They started for the Carolina slave market. Oar had already provided a place for Paulette, to which she was taken. Her most trying moment for her was when she watched her mother and sister climb into the cage.

CHAPTER 2

THE SLAVE TRADER

Jester Windborne was from the north, he had come south to make a living selling slaves. A more horrible disgusting looking person couldn't be found anywhere. Tall, lean, and lanky, with gray eyes, sandy hair and bushy eyebrows, and a long shabby sandy beard. He took pride in what he called his goodness of heart, and was always speaking of his compassion for others. He was determined to leave Cape Charles early in the morning. In this endeavor he was most successful, not even Paulette who had tried to talk to her mother and sister; was aware of the time that they were to leave. The slave-trader started out a little after midnight, and had loaded his human cargo a ships to Norfolk, long before most people were out of their beds.

Some slave thought living on a plantation in the Deep South was worse than death. Some of them were looking for an opportunity to escape. Jester was aware of this; he put chains on all the slaves before they set out on their journey. When they reached Charlotte, he ordered men to be chained in pairs, and the women were allowed to travel unchained. After a little more than thirty days, the company arrived on the banks of the Catawba River, not far from Charlotte North Carolina. They marched along a stream to enter South Carolina; from there they took a ship to Atlanta Georgia. Before they reached Atlanta, the Atlanta Tribune ran a full page article stating

9

that a prime lot of able-bodied slaves. Men and women, for field-work, with a few redbones trained as house-servants, all between the ages of thirteen and thirty.

After the ship had left the pier approaching the deeper waters of the Atlantic, Jester called his servant Edgar to his cabin; and ordered him to get the cargo ready for market. The slaves that Jester was going to sell were older ones. Slave so old that you could tell they had lived for many years. He ordered their gray hair to be died to make them look around the ages stated in the Tribunes advertisement. Edgar had worked for Windborne for years, he knew the business well, but he didn't enjoy doing it.

Eddo, he was usually called by the trader, was of African blood, and would often say, when talking to himself, "I'm from Angola, and I am African, not a Negro. I am all African. I am from Angola, not like mixed-breed Negro's bornrn on plantations."

Edgar was of low stature, round face, and, had a set of beautiful white teeth; his eyes were large, lips thick, and hair short and woolly. Edgar had been with Windborne so long, and had seen so much of buying and selling of slaves, that he appeared perfectly indifferent to the heart-rending scenes.

Watching slaves being treated like domesticated animals. He refused to get familiar with them. First he endured, then slowly shame showed on his face, he embraced his people. It was on the second day after the ship's voyage, Edgar selected five of the oldest slaves; he took them into a room and prepared them for market.

How old is you?" he asked a man older than forty.

"If I live to see next sweet-potato-digging time, I be fifty, I think."

"You may be," replied Edgar; "but now you is only thirty two years old...That's what master says you is to be."

"I is more then that," responded the man.

"I don't care," grumbled Edgar; "when you get in the market and any one ask you how old you is, tell 'em you is forty, or master will tie you up and cut you all to pieces; you is thirty years old."

"Well then, I be thirty."

"What's your name?" said Edgar, speaking to another and than another.

"Eric."

"Oh! Uncle Jim, is it?"

"Yes."

"Shave off all them gray whiskers, and shave your head."

"How old is you?" asked Edgar of a tall, Masai, looking man.

"What's your name?"

"I am twenty-nine years old, and my names is Percy, but call me P. J."

"Well, P. J., or Percy, you are twenty-five years old; that's all...do you understand that?"

"Yes," replied Percy.

Edgar now had made them all understand how old they were to be when asked by persons who might be interested in purchasing, and then went and reported to his boss that the older slaves were all right.

"Make sure," said Windborne, "that those niggers don't forget what you've told them. This time our luck in the market depends up-on their appearance. If any of them have a gray hair...take your knife and shave it off, and if he resist...beat him."

Late in the evening of the third day, lights of another ship were seen in the distance, and coming up very fast. This was the warning sign of a commotion on board the Southern Bell, and every-thing indicated that a boat-race was at hand. Nothing could exceed the excitement you got watching ships race on the Atlantic. By the time the boats reached mid stream they were side by side, and each trying take the lead. The night was clear, the moon shining brightly, and the boats so near to each other that the passengers were shouting at each other. On board the Southern Bell the firemen were using oil, lard, butter, and even bacon grease, with wood, for the purpose of raising the steam to its highest point. The flames mingled with the gray smoke that surged from the pipes of the other ship, which showed that she also was burning something more combustible than wood.

The firemen of both boats, who were slaves, were singing songs that could only be heard on board a Southern ship. The boats now came abreast of each other, and nearer and nearer, until they were so close that men could step from one to the other. The wildest excitement prevailed among the men employed on the ships, in which the passengers freely mingled with. The Southern Bell stopped to take in passengers, but still no steam was permitted to escape. On the starting of the boat again, cold water was forced into the boilers by feed-pumps, and, one of its boilers exploded, destroying the boiler-room and ripping huge holes in the engine. Steam resembling dense fog surged over the ship, while screams, groans, and cries were heard on every side.

Men were running around looking for their wives, and women were dashing about in confusion looking for their husbands. Panic and fear was on every face. The bar and cabins soon looked more like hospitals than anything else; but by this time the Southern Bell had drifted to the shore, and the other ship had come alongside to give assistance to the disabled boat. The dead and wounded, twenty in number, were taken on shore, and the Southern Bell, towed by the Savannah, had taken on its last journey.

Liberty Dendron

It was half-past twelve, and the passengers, instead of retiring to their beds, assembled at the gambling-tables. Thousands of dollars change hands. "Go call my son, I mean my servant," said Mr. Malloy, as he took his cards one by one from the table." In a few minutes a fine-looking, bright-eyed mulatto boy, about sixteen years of age, was standing by his master's side at the table.

"I am broke, all but my boy," said Malloy, running his fingers through his cards; "he is worth more than a thousand dollars and I'll bet all of it."

"Call you," said McKinney, laying five hundred dollars at the feet of the boy, who was standing on the table; and at the same time throwing down his cards before his adversary.

"You have beaten me," said Malloy; and a roar of laughter followed from the other gentleman as Jeffrey stepped down from the table.

"Well, I suppose I owe you half the nigger," said McKinney, as he took hold of Jeffrey and began examining his limbs.

"Yes," replied Malloy, "he is yours. Give me five hundred dollars, and I'll give you a bill of sale."

"Go to bed boy," said McKinney to his slave, "remember that you belong to me now."

The slave wiped the tears from his eyes, and in obedience, he turned to leave the table.

"He's my son," said Malloy, as he took the money, "and I hope, Mr. McKinney, that you will allow me to redeem him."

"Most certainly, sir," replied McKinney. "When ever you give me a thousand dollars, the Nigger is yours."

The next morning, as the passengers were assembling in the cabin and on deck, and while the slaves were running about waiting on or looking for their masters, Jeffrey was seen entering his new master's stateroom, boots in hand.

"Who do you belong to?" inquired an old Negro, who passed along leading a Pointer dog which he had been feeding.

"When I went to sleep last night," replied the slave, "I longed to Master' Byrd; but he's bin gambl' all night, I don't know who I longs to this morning."

On the fourth morning, the Southern Bell landed at Jacksonville. Among the passengers boarding was another slave-trader, with slaves he was taking to market. The passengers, both ladies and gentlemen, were startled when they saw a slave, so white that couldn't be distinguishable from the other white people on board. She was in chains. In her arms she held a child so white; no one would think African blood flowed through its veins.

There she sat, with a face full of dignity without fear, her dark golden locks rolled back from her pearly white forehead and floating over her bosom. The stare that stood in her calm blue eyes, revealed that she was in deep thought. When the ship arrived at Miami, a rather good-looking, man came on board to purchase a servant. This individual introduced himself to Windborne as the Rev. Mucky Hall. The slave-trader escorted the preacher to the lower deckwhere he kept his slaves, and the man of God, after having some questions answered, selected Maggie as the one best suited to his needs.

It seemed as if Jessica's heart would break when she realized that she was to be separated from her mother. The preacher, however, appeared to be but little moved by their sorrow, and took his newly-purchased slave on shore. Maggie begged him to buy her daughter, but he refused. During the remainder of the passage, Jessica wept. After a run of a few hours, the boat stopped at Tampa, where more passengers boarded, among whom were a number of persons who had gone to Tampa to see the horse race. Gambling and drinking were now the order of the day. The next morning, at ten o'clock, the boat arrived at Tallahassee, where most of the passengers went to their homes and slaves to the slave-pens.

CHAPTER 3

SLAVES AND PREACHERS

Not far from where the ship docked, in the city of Tallahassee, stood a large two-story white building, surrounded by a brick wall nearly ten feet high, the top of which is covered with barbwire, to prevent any one from climbing over it. The rooms in this building resemble the cells of a prison, and in a small apartment near the "office" were iron collars, hobbles, handcuffs, thumbscrews, cowhides, chains, gags, and yokes. The back-yard was enclosed by a high wall, it looked like a school playground, in which are rows of benches and swings. In the back of the building sat a kitchen, where, two old Negro women were working, scattering something carelessly over the floor, boiling, and baking, and occasionally wiping perspiration from their foreheads.

Windborne stayed the night with his slaves, the next morning at eight thirty; the slaves were on exhibit for sale. The first slave to mount the auction block was Jessica, whose pale face and sad look revealed how many unhappy hours had passed since parting with her mother at Hicksville. And there, too, was a woman who had been separated from her husband; and another woman, whose looks and manners were that of deep anguish, who sat by her side. There stood "Uncle Eric," with his whiskers gone, his face shaven clean, and all his

15

hair shaved off his head, ready to be sold for years younger than he was. Percy was also there, with his face shaved and greased, ready for inspection.

The examination started. "What are you wiping your eyes for?" inquired a fat, red-faced man, with a straw hat set on one side of his head and a cigar in his mouth.

"I left my man behind."

"Oh, if I buy you, I'll give you a man to sleep with. I've got lots of young bucks on my plantation."

"I'll never sleep with another man," replied the woman.

"What's you name?" asked a tall muscular Negro who stood with his arms folded across his chest, leaning against the wall.

"My name is Grady, sir."

"How old are you?"

"Twenty-seven."

"Where were you raised?"

"Virginia, on the eastern shores, sir."

"How many men have owned you?"

"Five"

"Are you in good health?"

"Yes, sir."

"How long did you live with your first owner?"

"Twenty years."

"Did you ever run away?"

"No, sir."

"Did you ever strike your master?"

"No, sir."

"Were you whipped much?"

"No, sir; I suppose I didn't need it, sir."

"How long did you live with your master?"

"Ten years, sir."

"Have you a good appetite?"

"Yes, sir."

"Can you eat no more than you earn?"

"Yes, sir, I'd have too."

"Where did you say you worked and lived in Virginia?"

"On the Bush Plantation, in Cape Charles. I worked in the tobacco field."

"The tobacco field, eh?"

"Yes, sir."

"How old did you say you are?"

"Be twenty-seven, sir, sweet potato diggin' time."

"If I buy you, you'll work in cotton-field."

My men pick one hundred and fifty pounds a day and the women one hundred and forty pound. Those who fail to perform get struck with a wet rawhide whip, five times, for each pound unpicked. Do you think you can keep up with the rest of the hands?"

"I don't know, sir, somehow I'd have to."

"How long did you live with your master?"

"Three years, sir."

"Why, that makes you over thirty. I thought you told me you were only twenty-seven?"

Grady looked at the plantation owner, then at the slave trader, and gazed straight ahead confused. The plantation owner questions had confused Edgar.

"Let me see your back, than I'll know how much you've been whipped, before I buy you."

Edgar, who had been standing by during the examination, thought that his services were now required, and, stepping forth with a degree of officiousness, said to Grady. "Didn't you hear the man say he wants to see your back? Take off your shirt now."

Grady was examined, and pronounced sound; even with the conflicting statement about his age. Fortunately for Jessica, she was spared the pain of undergoing such an examination. Mr. Doberman a teller in one of the banks, had just gotten married, and wanted a servant for his wife.

The Rev. Mucky Hall had barely finished his education at the University of Main, when he was invited by his uncle to visit his home in Atlanta. Young Hall accepted his uncle's invitation, and accompanied him to the South. Living in Atlanta he became a popular preacher, and built a large congregation.

Mr. Hall had hired an overseer to run his farm, Vernon Knox, a man with a good reputation. The Hall Farm was located in a beautiful valley, nine miles from Hicksville. It was nearly thirty, long, miles from the Atlantic Ocean.

It was in the kitchen of this house that Maggie found her new home. Mr. Hall was every inch a republican, and early resolved that "his people," as he called his slaves, should be well-fed and not overworked, and therefore laid down the law and gospel to the overseer as well as to the slaves. "It is my wish," said he to Mr. Grimily, an old school-fellow who was spending a few days with him.

"It is my wish that a new system be adopted on plantations in souther states. I believe that the sons of God should obey the gospel. The gospel was written to make mankind better and no one should be without it."

"What say you," said Grimily, "about the right of man to his liberty?"

"Now, Grimily, you have begun to talk again about men's rights. I really wish that you could see this matter as I do."

"I regret that I cannot see eye to eye with you," said Grimily.

Liberty Dendron

"I am a disciple of God, and have for years made the rights of man my study, I confess to you that I see no difference between white and black, as it regards liberty."

"Now, my dear Grimily, do you really want Negroes to enjoy the same rights as ourselves?"

"Most certainly. Read the Declaration of Independence! Read the Constitution of our own home state Main, and see what is said in these great documents about liberty."

"I hate all this talk about rights. The Bible is older than the Declaration of Independence."

A long discussion followed, in which both gentlemen put forth their unconventional ideas with compassion. During this conversation, there was another person in the room, seated by the window, who, although at work, embroidering a fine collar, paying little attention to what was said. This was Tonya, the daughter of the man, who had just returned from Main, where she had finished her education. She had studied the contrasting argument of Christianity and liberty in other countries with that of slavery in her native United States, and had begun to feel deeply about the injustice forced on Negro.

Tonya was twenty years old, and had learned many different things, when visiting her relatives in the North. She was tall and graceful, her features regular, but well-defined, and her complexion was illuminated by the freshness of youth, beauty, and health. Her thoughts differed from both her father and his friend on the subject which they had been discussing; and as soon as an opportunity came, she said that the Bible supported Christianity and liberties. With a smile she said..."My father is confused, like many of us that have been reared in the south. I am a native of the South, but I have the com-passion, and kindness of my northern relatives."

Mr. Hall laughed, appearing rather pleased than otherwise at the manner in which his daughter had expressed herself. From this Tonya took courage and continued. Saying. *"Thou shall love thy neighbor as thyself.* Tonya, you are an abolitionist...you're against slavery!" said Mr. Hall, in rather a sharp tone, but the subdued look of the woman and the presence of Grimily caused him to soften his language.

Mr. Hall having lost his wife by a contagious disease, and Tonya being his only child, he loved her too dearly to say more, even if he disagreed. A silence followed the exchange of words from the young Christian woman, but her remarks had struck a brutal blow. Her Father's heart was touched, and the skeptic, for the first time, was viewing Christianity in its true light.

Besides Maggie, whom Mr. Hall had purchased from the slave-trader, Windborne, there were other house-servants. The main servant was Travis, who was second in control. They were planning a party; the people to be invited were sent invitations. The arrangements had been made by the minister and his daughter. Travis was asked for his advice by Miss Hinson. The name the servants used when addressing Miss Hall. If anything was to be purchased, Travis felt that he had been snubbed if his opinion was not asked. As to the marketing, he did it. He sat at the head of the servants' table in the kitchen, and was a big wheel at his church. A slight glance from him was enough to silence any conversation among the servants in the kitchen or in any other part of the mansion.

Travis was originally from Bermuda, and through the action of one of his young masters, whom he had to escort to school, he learned to read while looking in the window and listen to everything that was to the students. He was so smart that he was called a genius, not only among slaves, but also by those who knew him. Travis wanted to be a scientist. But there was a problem. Travis was a Negro. This he evidently regarded as a great misfortune; but he endeavored to make up for it in dress. Mr. Hall kept his house-servants well dressed, and as for Travis, he was seldom seen except in a ruffled shirt. The servants feared him more than any one else in the house.

Maggie was in charge of all the going owns in the kitchen, and helped with supervision of the household affairs. Jamul, the coachman, Kawaka, and Bamako made up the remainder of the house-servants. Besides these, Mr. Hall owned eight slaves who were masons, they also worked in town and on other plantations. Every Sunday evening, Mr. Hall's servants, including the more skilled workers met in the kitchen, where the events of the week were fully discussed and commented upon. It was on a Sunday evening, in the month of June, that there was a party at Mr. Hall's house, the ladies had their maid-servants with them. Tea had been served in the main house, now the house servants, including the servants of the guest, had taken a seat at the table in the kitchen. Travis, flirted with female servants on these occasions.

Daily Travis brushed his hair. He thought that carrot oil was better for his hair than any kind of grease. When guest came to the plantation, he would oil his hair; and put a moisturizing ointment on his face to keep his skin from drying out, in the blistering sun. Therefore, on the evening of the party, when all the servants were at the table, Travis stood out. There he sat, with his hair well combed and extremely clean face, in his white ruffled shirt. A preacher in his drawing-room did not make a more imposing appearance than did

Travis on those occasions.

"I had my fortune told last Sunday," said Travis, while helping one of the girls.

"Indeed!" cried half a dozen voices.

"Yes," continued he; "Carmel told me I would marry, and that

21

I will someday be free!"

All eyes were immediately turned toward Leticia Featherstone, who was seated near Travis.

"I see somebody blushing at that remark," said Jamul.

"Pass the pancakes and molasses, Mr. Kramer."

"That reminds me," said Maggie, "that Dora Ricardo is going to get married."

"Who to?" ask Kawaka.

"To one of Mr. Braziers' field-hands," answered Maggie.

"That girl could do better," said Adie. She's good looking, she doesn't have to marry a field hand.

"Yes," said Travis, "you're right, Miss Adie. There are plenty of capable well-dressed house-servants that a gal of her looks can get rather than marring one of those common darkies."

The evening's entertainment concluded by Travis talking about his experience with his first master in Bermuda. This master was a doctor, and had a large practice among his neighbors, doctoring both masters and slaves. When Travis was about fifteen years old, his master let him grind roots, make ointment, and pills. As he grew older and became more knowledgeable, his services were even more importance to the doctor. The physician having a good business, and a large number of his patients being slaves, taught Travis the art of bleeding, pulling teeth, and had him practicing medicine to slaves. Travis soon acquired the name among the slaves of the Black Doctor. With this title he was delighted; and no regular physician could have put on more airs than did Travis when his services were required. He examined his patients more toughly than the doctor.

On one occasion the doctor was ill, and unable to go to his patients. A slave with pass in hand, came to the plantation to receive medical advice, the master sent Travis to examine the man and to see what was needed. This delighted Travis beyond measure, because he had never been asked before to examine a white patient. This convinced him that he was a doctor. He put on a convincing show when examining the man. Standing in front of his patient, folding his arms across his chest.

"Where do you hurt?"

"All over."

"Exactly where?"

"Here," replied the man, putting his hand on his stomach.

"Put out your tongue," continued Travis.

The man pushed out his tongue.

"Let me feel your pulse;" at the same time taking his patient's hand in his, and placing a fingers upon his pulse, he said..."Ah! If something not done, right away, you'll die."

The plantation owner was afraid, and asked what was wrong with him.

Travis said. "I told you you're very sick, that's all you need to know."

When Travis returned to his master, he asked. "Travis what do you think is wrong?"

"His stomach is out of order, sir," he replied.

"What do you think should be done?"

"I should bleed him and give him a dose of laxative," said Travis. The master let him do what he thought was right.

On another occasion, while making pills and ointment, Travis made an awful mistake. After walking to the door to greet a patient; his master picked the preparations and put it in the wrong place, now both were mixed together, so that he couldn't make either. Fearing that if he threw the stuff away, his master would whip him, and being afraid to inform his master of his mistake, he decided to make the whole batch pills and ointment stuff. He knew that the powder over the pills would hide the contents and the fact that most people shut their eyes when taking such a nasty tasting medicine he thought he would get away with it. Travis boxed them up, and labels them, and placed them on the shelf.

Travis felt a degree of anxiety about his deception. He knew it was a strange mixture, and he wasn't certain whether this mixture would kill or cure, but he had a feeling that it would be alright. Col. Springfield, one of Dr. Woodruff's patients, came to the plantation one morning, and Travis ran out to hold the colonel's horse.

"Call your master," said the colonel.

The doctor walked over to the carriage, and inquired about the health of his patient. After a brief conversation, the doctor returned to his office, took down a box of pills, and returned to the carriage.

"Take two of these every morning and night," said the doctor, "and if you don't get any relief, double the dose."

"My gracious," exclaimed Travis in an undertone, when he heard his master tell the colonel how to take the pills. It was several days before Travis heard the result of his new medicine. One after-noon, after the colonel's visit, Travis saw Col. Springfield riding up to the gate on horseback. The doctor was in the yard; he met the colonel and asked. "How are you feeling?"

"I've recovered," he replied. "Those pills of yours made me feel better the next day."

"I knew they would," said the doctor.

Travis was near enough to hear the conversation, and was de-lighted beyond description. He walked into the kitchen, and sat in a chair.

"What the matter with you?" asked the cook.

"I'm the best doctor in his country," replied Travis. "If you get

24

sick, call me. No matter what ails you, I'll help you; I've invented a medicine that can cure you in no time. If you have a backache, head-ache, rheumatics, anything, I'm the man that can cure you." For weaks, Travis did little more than boast of his skill as a doctor. He was always the first man in all the Negro balls and parties. When his mas-ter gave him a pass he went to the party. When he didn't give him one, he sneaked away after his master went to bed, running the risk of being caught by the night-watch. At night it was his duty to put out the lights, and clean his master's boots, and hang his clothes in the closete until the morning; and take the boots back to his master's room the next morning.

He decided to attend a dress-ball one night, and dressed up in Mr. Woodruff's clothes, even his boots and hat; off he started for the party. The next morning, Travis was home long before Mr. Hall got up, and the clothes were put in the closet. For a weeks Travis had didn't have a problem dressing for parties. One night Mr. Woodruff heard a knock at the door. He lit a lantern and looked for his clothes, they were gone. It was twelve o'clock, and his clothes, hat, boots, and even his watch, couldn't be found.

Here was a puzzling situation for him to be in. It took a while for Mr. Woodruff to dress him self to make the visit. He started out with one of the farm-horses, because Travis had taken his horse and saddle. He was certain that Travis had robbed him, and was on his way to Mexico. He didn't know, Travis had gone to another plantation to attend a ball, in his best suit. Mr. Woodruff returned before morn-ing, and went to bed but with little hope of sleep; his thoughts were on finding Travis and his horse. At six o'clock, in walked Travis with his clothes, and his boots polished. He placed the watch back on the shelf, and the hat in its place.

"What have you been doing——and where were you last night

when I called you?" Asked Mr. Woodruff.

"I don't know, sir. I was asleep," replied Travis.

Mr. Woodruff knew he was lying. After breakfast, Travis was taken into the barn, tied up, and severely beaten with a wet rawhide whip, and he told the truth; He was no longer allowed to practice medicine.

CHAPTER 4

STERNER HOVER

Sterner Hover purchered Jessica, he was from the cold climate of Minneapolis, his feelings were not in support of the holding of slaves; but his wife convinced him that that it was no worse to own a slave than to hire one and pay the money to someone else.

Clyde Verso, a physician from Minneapolis had just started practicing medicine in Tallahassee, was boarding with Hover when Jessica was brought home. The young physician had been in Folrida only a few weeks, and had seen only uneducated slaves. In Minneapolis he had been taught that slaves of the Southern States were uneducated Negroes, and they were not like Africans from the coast of Africa. He was unprepared to meet Jessica, who had been sold as livestock. He shivered while listening to Sterner Hover brag about how he bartered with the slave trader, and he bought her for three hundred dollars less than the slave trader had asked. The expression on his face revealed his dislike of slavery.

Jessica had been brought up by her mother to look after the

domestic concerns of her log cabin in Virginia; she knew how to per-form domestic duties. Mrs. Hover was very pleased with her new servant, and often mentioned her good qualities in the presence of Mr. Verso. After months of knowing Jessica, Verso's sympathies changed to love. He bought her, and made her his wife after moving to Mobile Alabama, where Jessica passed for white.

In no time at all, Dr. Verso built a large and influential prac-tice, and with it increased in wealth; but with all his wealth he never owned a slave. In Alabama Jessica tried to purchase her mothers free-dom, from Mucky Hall, at Hicksville. But her efforts had come too late; her mother died of a fever before the arrival of her husband's agent. Clyde Verso was a kind and affectionate husband; and his wish to purchase her mother, although unsuccessful, had made Jessica love him even more. Nearly a year had passed after their marriage; Jessica gave her husband a lovely daughter, who bought them even closer to-gether. They named the child Brenda; and before the second year ended, they had another daughter, whom they named Cathy. And at the ages of ten and eleven, the girls were sent north to finish their education.

In Cape Charles was a fancy log cabins surrounded by trees, which cabin could only be seen from the Chesapeake Bay. Beyond the trees was the road. This was where Kenneth Oar had built a cabin for Paulette. He had his most trusted slaves to build this cabin on his fa-ther's plantation. He furnished it and Paulet lived there. When Kenneth was not with her, she was busy working in her Garden planting flowers. She planted in front of her cabin: Roses, lilies, glad-iolus, iris, morning-glory, and other plants that grew in Virginia.

Paulette had been told by Kenneth that she would be free someday, and that he would always consider her as his wife. She wanted to get married but he would never consider marrying a slave.

Human Cattle

Here, in this secluded grove, unvisited by any other except her lover, Paulette lived for years. Now she was the mother of a lovely daughter, named Paula. The complexion of the child was even fairer than her mothers. And fairer than most white children, as she grew older she looked just like her father.

As time passed, Kenneth stopped visiting Paulette and his child, weeks and even months passed without them seeing him, or knowing where he was. Becoming more acquainted with the world outside his fathers plantation, and dating women of his own station, Paulette had become a burden, and having satisfied his desires, he wanted to free himself of this responsibility; but when he looked at his child, he felt that he owed her something.

Kenneth was now a Senitor, in his contact with his new friends he had started dating Loretta Cavalla, the daughter of a wealthy gentleman who lived in Maryland. Lest than a mile from he Virginia border. Instead of finding fault with the infrequent visits of Kenneth, Paulette always greeted him with a smile, and tried to make herself believe that business was the cause of his negligence.

Paula loved her father so much; she gazed at her father with tears in her eyes, and watched his every move. But he had no time for her. His heart had grown hard. He and Loretta had been married for nearly two years before Paulette was told, and that was by accident.

One afternoon, Paulette and Paula were picking berries near the road a carriage drove past. Paulet turned her face to keep from being seen by strangers, not knowing that it was Kenneth and his wife. Paula, new the carriage, and screamed at the top of her voice, "Papa! Papa!" Her mother turned to look at the strangers, and her eyes met those of Kenneth. Loretta's eyes were on Paula. The swiftness with which Kenneth drove by could not hide the striking resemblance of the child calling him. And she had heard so clearly Paula shouting "Papa! Papa!" and she noticed by the shame and quivering of his lips. The nervousness of his body and the frown on his face, that something was wrong.

"Who is that woman? And why did that child call you papa?" she asked, with a shivering voice.

Kenneth was silent; he didn't know what to say, without a word, they drove home. Upon reaching her home Loretta rushed into her room, she wiped her face with her handkerchief as she wept. When they went to bed that night, the problems of the day followed them. The beauty of Paulette, with her flowing long curly hair, and the look of the child, resembling the man whom she so dearly loved, could not be forgotten; and the sound of the child's voice screaming, "Papa! Papa!" rang in her ears all night. And the return of her husband after twelve that night didn't help the situation. Feeling his guilt, he had gotten out of bed and left the house.

The night was dark, rain poured, from huge gray overhanging Clouds. Thunder echoed off the Chesapeake Bay and flashes of lightning shattered trees and they fell with vengeance, as Kenneth stepped from his carriage and entered Paulette's cabin. More than 14 days had passed since the accidental meeting, and Paulette didn't know who the woman was that Kenneth was with in the carriage. She had no idea that it was his wife. With a smile, Paulette met her lover as he entered her cabin. Paula had gone to bed, but her father's voice woke her from her sleep, and she was soon sitting on his knee.

His face revealed his uneasiness. Paulette smiles and laughed and asked, "That lady was one of your relatives?" led him to assume that she was still in ignorance of his marriage. She didn't know who the lady was. Being aware of this, he now acted more like himself, and treated the encounter as a joke. But in her heart, Paulette felt uneasy and the uneasiness showed. With a great effort, she aid..."Kenneth, if I am in the way of your future happiness, say so, and I will release you from any promises that you have made me. I know there is no law by which I can hold you, and if there was, I wouldn't. You are as dear to me as ever, and I'll always be devoted to you. It's a great sacrifice for me to give you up to another, but if it's your desire, I will. Send me and your child north to a free state if we're in your way."

Again and again he told Paulet that no other woman had his love but her. The intense storm kept Kenneth from returning home until well after two. As he drew near his mansion he saw his wife standing near the window. He entered the house, and found his wife in tears. Although he had never explained to Loretta who the slave woman and child were, he held her in his arms and told her that she was mistaken, and that she thought she heard the child calling him "papa." He said that he had been caught in the rain while out, which kept him from returning sooner. She belived him.

Now drunk, from drinking brandy, and tired, Kenneth fell to sleep as soon as he hit the bed. But Loretta couldn't sleep. With anxiety, she watched him, thrashing and talking in his sleep. Again and again he said Paulette, and more than once she heard him say, "I am not married; I will never marry while you are alive." Then he would say "Paula, My child, I love you!"

After a sleepless night, Loretta arose from the couch, determined to talk to her mother about this affair. Mrs. Cavalla was a woman of little or no feeling, proud, bad-tempered, and passionate, she made everybody miserable that came near her. When she disliked someone, her hatred had no bounds. The Next day, Loretta went to Maryland to visit her mother and told her what had happened. Mrs. Cavalla angrily yell at Loretta for not having told her sooner, and was determined to find out who the woman and child were.

For weeks Mrs. Cavalla visited the Oar Plantation, questioning house servants and field slaves, trying to find out who this woman was, but without success. Six weeks passed, the fiery of the Mrs. Cavalla's temper had calmed down. Then, one evening, as she was approaching her daughter's mansion, she saw Kenneth riding in the direction of where the woman and her child lived. She followed him. His horse's hooves pounded the ground so loudly that she had no problem following him without being seen.

After a ride of about ten miles, Kenneth turned into a narrow camouflaged rugged road, lest than fifty feet away was a cabin. It was a foggy starlight night, and the moon was rising when they got to their journey's end. As usual, Paulette met Kenneth with a smile, and expressed her fears regarding his health. Hours passed, and still Mrs. Cavalla hid in the woods near the house, determined to know who lived there. The moon had risen, it was casting its beams upon the cabin as Kenneth stepped from Paulette's door, looking at his watch, and said, "I must go, sweetheart; it's half-past ten."

Had Paula been awake, she too would have been at the door. As Kenneth walked to the gate, Paulette followed with her left hand locked in his. Again he looked at her, and said, "I must go."

"It been more than two years since you staid all night," said Paulette, as he held her gently in his arms, kissing her.

He was nearly out of sight when, Paulette stepped on the porch and started to open the door. Paula woke up when the door squiked and asked her mother how long her father had been gone. At that moment a knock was heard at the door. Thinking that it was Kenneth returning for something he had forgotten, Paulette rushed to let him in. To her amazement, it was a strange woman standing in the door.

"Who are you that come here at this hour of night?" demanded the Paulette.

Without making any reply, Mrs. Cavalla pushed Paulette aside, and stepped in the house.

"What do you want?" Demanded Pulette.

"I've come to see you," Mrs. Cavalla said calmly; thinking that her visit would serve its purpose better, if she were kind.

Mrs. Cavalla was trying to find out the connection that existed between Kenneth and Paulette, and after probing all she could out of Paulette, she told her that Kenneth was married. Shocked and caught off guard, Paulette fainted and fell upon the floor. How long she remained there she didn't know; but when she regained consciousness, the woman was gone, Paula was kneeling by her side shaking her.

When she recovered enough to stand, Paulette went to the door, and walked into the yard, she saw that the woman was gone. standing in the yard the moon cast its ray over her, giving her an innocent appearance. Suddenly another change came over her, and her lips trembled with suppressed emotion. The muscles around her mouth quiver, she gasped and tried to breave, and cried out, "why!" and fainted again.

Paula rushed to her mother and sprinkled cold water on her mother's face to bring her too.

The night passed, but without sleep for Paulette. As the sun rose, she tried to make herself believe that what, had happened last night was a dream.

CHAPTER 5

MRS. CARVELLA

When Kenneth returned home, he found his wife sitting at the window, awaiting his approach. Grief beyond understanding feeling were controlling her thoughts. Her sunken cheeks and puffy eyes showed her agony, far deeper than her speech could ever do. A dull and deadly silence lingered in the room. His face slumped and the hairs on the back of his neck stood up. Feeling that were so very clear too see, Loretta was up set; she knew he had a secret lover. The curtains were pushed open to let the light of the moon shine in the room. The grandfather clock in the vestibule, struck the hour of twelve, as Kenneth sat by the side of Loretta, his devoted and loving wife; he asked how she was feeling.

"I'm okay, Kenneth," replied Loretta; "but you're not."

"Why?" he inquired.

"Because of that look in your eyes." she replied.

He protested his innocence, vowing she was the only woman.

Kenneth and Loretta were rising from the breakfast-table the next morning when Mrs. Cavalla walked in. She immediately took her daughter aside, and told her what happened last night, telling her how she followed Kenneth to Paulete's cabin, describing and telling each and ever element of her conversation with Paulette. Mrs. Cavalla urged her daughter to demand that the slave and her child be at once sold and taken to the Deep South. "Assert your rights, my dear. Don't share your husband with anyone...especially a slave," said Mrs. Cavalla, with anger in her eyes. "Don't go to bed tonight, my child, until that woman has been removed from that cottage. The child, give her to me."

During these remarks, Mrs. Cavalla was pacing up and down the room like a caged animal. Paulette had told her that, she had been purchased by Kenneth, and he is the father of her child. While Mrs. Cavalla was shouting and telling her daughter about her rights and duties, Kenneth, unaware of what was going on, had left the house and gone to his office. As soon as Mrs. Cavalla realized that he was gone, she said... "I will bet anything that he is on his way to see that slave girl. I'll bet my life on it."

The entrance, of Yakima, asking for Master Oar's saddle bag, informed her that her son-in-law was at his office. Before Mrs. returned home to Maryland, it was agreed that Loretta should come to her mother's plantation for tea that evening, and Kenneth with her and that Mrs. Cavalla would confront Kenneth about his infidelity to her daughter, and insist on the immediate removal of Paulette. With this understanding, Mrs. Cavalla returned home. On the borders of Virginia and Maryland, sheltered by large pine oak and willow trees was the plantation where Mrs. Cavalla lived. There was an orchard in the rear of the house, and the old weather-beaten White Oak and Dog Wood trees, with "moss-covered branches" in the back yard, branches swinging majestically over the deep stream. The garden was scarcely to be equaled. Its grounds were laid out in excellent taste, and rare exotic plants in the greenhouse.

It was a breezy autumn evening, the air rushed through the open window, as the sun set, cardinals and orioles perched on grapes vines. Then Kenneth and Loretta were seen approaching the mansion in an enclosed carriage; it was nothing more than a pleasant ride through the country side. The parlor was surrounded on all sides with windows, and the sun creeping through the curtains.

It was in this room that Loretta first met Kenneth, and the pleasant hours she had spent there with him were comparable to none. It was here that, her radiant beauty made her seem as fascinating and as lovely as that of any fancy woman. Her sweet, soft voice could easily be heard in every part of this huge mansion, occasionally surprising you with an unexpected touch. Her beautiful face, and shapely figure, couldn't be painted by the greatest artist; to do her justice. Now she sat in this room...with a broken heart.

The servants in the kitchen were delighted when they were told that "Miss Loretta," as they called their young mistress, was in the house. She saved them from many a flogging, by interceding for them, when her mother was in one of her uncontrollable modes. Lynn, the cook, always expected Miss Loretta to visit the kitchen as soon as she came, and was unhappy, on this occasion, at what she considered her young mistress's neglect. Uncle Frog, also, expected her to visit the green house, and, congratulate him on his job as a gardener.

When tea was over, Mrs. Cavalla told the servants to leave the room. Then she told her son-in-law what she saw last night, and demanded that Paulette should be sent out of the State. To be certain that it was done; she wanted him to let her sell Paulette and Paula. Loretta was Mrs. Cavalla's only child, and Kenneth didn't want to put her or her mother threw more anguish. And long wishing to free himself from Paulette, he yielded to the demands of his mother-in-law. Mr. Cavalla was an extremely happy with his decision. If any one wanted to discuss business about the plantation, he would say, "Wait until I talk with my wife," and whatever his wife decided was done.

Mr. Cavalla never said a word, he wasn't prepared to criticize or find any faults in his son-in-law. It was settled that Mrs. Cavalla should use her own good judgment in removing Paulette from her cabin. With this understanding Kenneth and Loretta went home. Kenneth wanted to see Paulette once more, to tell her to run for her life; but fearing the wrath of Mrs. Cavalla, he didn't dare. He didn't know what would happen to them, but he knew Mrs. Cavalla would have no mercy.

While seated in her bedroom with her face hidden in her handkerchief, Paula ran in excitedly and told her mother that a carriage stopped in front of the house. With a broken heart she arose from her bed and went to the door. The woman who had come to her home, the evening that she had last seen Kenneth, stepped out of the carriage, accompanied by the slave-trader, Windborne. Paulette had seen Windborne when he purchased her mother and sister, and recognized him. Why are these people here? She was thinking. Without saying a word, they entered the house, leaving the carriage in charge of a servant.

Paula ran to her mother, and clung to her dress frightened by the strangers.

"She's a fine-looking woman," said the slave trader, as he seated himself, unasked, in the rocking-chair; "but I don't think she is worth the money you're asking for her."

"Why have you come here?" asked Paulette, with a quivering voice.

"Shut up," shouted Cavalla, at the top of her voice; "if you say another word, I'll give you a good whipping."

In agony, pale, trembling, and ready to sink to the floor, Paulette was hoping that she would be able to save her child. Finally realizing what was happening, now thinking clearly, she told them to leave her house. Feeling insulted, Mrs. Cavalla picked up the fire-tong standing by the fire-place, and raised it to strike Paulette; but the slave-trader stepped between the women, exclaiming. "I won't buy her, Mrs. Cavalla, if you injure her." Paula screamed as she saw the strange woman raise the fire-tongs to strike her mother. With the exception of old Aunt Zephyr, a free colored woman, whom Paulette sometimes employed to work for her, Paula had never before seen a strange face in there house. Fearing that Paulette would resist, Mrs. Cavalla had ordered her overseer that controlled the slaves on her plantation to follow her; just as Windborne stepped between the two women, Mull, the Negro- driver, walked into the room.

"Seize that impudent hussy," said Mrs. Cavalla to the overseer, "and tie her up this minute, I'll teach her a lesson she won't forget."

As she spoke, her eyes rolled, her lips quivered, and face distorted...she looked and acted like a crazy woman.

"I will have nothing to do with her, if you whip her, Mrs. Cavalla," said the slave-trader. "She won't bring the price I need to get... People wont pay half of what a Niggers worth, no sir...don't bring half of what they're worth in the market...with their backs in strips," continued he, as the overseer followed Mrs. Cavalla's orders.

Paula reached for her father's walking-stick, which was lying on the sofa where he had left it, and, raising it, she said...

"If you bad people touch my mother, I will strike you."

They looked at the child with astonishment; and laughed.

"Oh, Kenneth, Kenneth!" exclaimed Paulette, wringing her hands while shaking her head.

"He can't help you, hussy; you'll never see him again," said Mrs. Cavalla.

"Is he dead?" asked Paulette.

It was then that she forgot her own situation, thinking only of the man she loved. Never having to endure any kind of abusive treatment, Paulette was not accustom to the brutality of Mrs. Cavalla. Or the brutality of her overseer. Instead of whipping Paulette, Mrs. Cavalla told the slave trader to take her, who took her immediately to his slave-pen.

Mrs. Cavalla shouted at Windborne. "I sold you her, not her things."

Paulette watched Paula struggling to get away from Mrs. Cavalla, and before she could move Mrs. Cavalla hit Paula with an open hand.

After leaving directions as to how Paulette's furniture and other things should be disposed of, Mrs. Cavalla ordered Paula into her carriage and drove home. A large commotion was created in the kitchen among the servants when the carriage drove up, and Paula entered the house.

"She looks just like Master Kenneth, can't see a drop of African blood," said Lynn, looking at Paula through the window.

"Wonder who's decided to bring her here?" said Brenda, as she put the tea in the pitchers for dinner."

That child looks white. What can be done to make her look like other Negroes was the question Mrs. Cavalla asked herself. The hard-hearted old woman bit her lip, as she watched Paula, standing before her, with her long, dark ringlets clustering over her snow- white brow and neck.

"Take this little nigger and cut her hair close to her head," said Mrs. Cavalla to Brenda, as another slave answered the bell. Paula screamed, when she felt the scissors cutting her hair, and saw her hair falling upon the floor. A roar of laughter burst from the servants, as Brenda led Paula through the kitchen, with the hair cut so short that her scalp could be seen.

"You look like us, now," said Lynn, smiling.

Mrs. Cavalla smiled, as Paula reentered the room; but there

was more needed to be done. The child was white, and that was her greatest objection. Nevertheless, she thought of a plan to cure that problem. It was hot. Not a cloud in the sky, or the slightest breeze. The earth was scorched by the broiling sun. Even the birds had stopped chirping. Bees had stopped humming, and butterflies were hiding under large flat leaves. Without a crumb to eat, Paula was put in the garden, and ordered to weed it. Her arms, neck, and head were completely bare. Not used to hard work, Paula wept as she pulled weeds. Old Lynn, the cook, was as unsympathetic as, Mrs. Cavalla, her mistress, she was happy when she saw Paula working in the hot sun. "That little white nigger will be blacker than I am, if she keeps working out there," she said, as she wiped the perspiration from her tan brow.

Lynn was the mother of fifteen children, all of whom had been taken from her when they were young; and this had harden her feelings, and make her hate all white people.

The burning sun poured its rays on the face Paula until she fainted and lay unconscious in the garden. She was being cooked in the broiling sun.

"That little red nigger ain't workin' Miss," said Lynn to Mrs. Cavalla, as she entered the kitchen.

"She's out there, lying in the sun. She'll work. I'll make sure of that," replied Mrs. Cavalla.

"These half-half-white niggers always think they're as good as white folks," said the cook.

"We'll teach them better, won't we, Lynn?" said Mrs. Cavalla.

"Yes, Miss," replied Lynn; "I don't like those half-white niggers. They think they're better than they are." With this remark the old cook laughed.

It was with the deepest humiliation that Kenneth had learned from one of his slaves. The treatment that his child was receiving at the hands of his mother-in-law. The scorching sun had given the desired effect; in less than four days, Paula could scarcely be recognized as the same child.

On Sunday's Mrs. Cavalla when to church and took Zephyr; or one of her servants to fan her during the service. Listening to the boring preacher, Zephyr would get sleepy and begin to nod. Often she would go to sleep. Which annoyed Mrs. Cavalla, with a pinch on Zephyr's arm, she would wake up. But there was none of Mrs. Cavalla's servants who was punished more than old Uncle Frog.

She was always punishing the old gardener. Uncle Frog was very religious, and, whenever Mrs. Cavalla flogged him he quoted scriptures from the Bible. Although unable to read, he remembered portions of Scripture, which he used whenever needed. In one end of the greenhouse was Uncle Frog's room, and those who happened to be in that area, between seven and eight at night they could hear the old man offering up his thanks to God for his protection, another day. Uncle Frog spoke loud and clear when he thought white folks were within hearing distance, when he was praying. Often he said, "O Lord, you know that white folks in the South, are not Christians, but black people are God's children." If Mrs. Cavalla could hear the sound of his voice, his words became clear and vicious.

It was on a chilly night, when the stars were casting a bright sheen, that Yakima and two of the other boys passed the greenhouse, and heard Uncle Frog praying.

"Let's have a little fun," said Yakima to his friend. "I'll make Uncle Frog believe that I am old mistress, and he'll give us a thrashing in his prayer." Yakima immediately started talking in a voice sounding like, Mrs. Cavalla, and at once Frog said in a loud voice, "O Lord, you know that white people are going to hell; but, as for old Frog, whenever the angel of the Lord comes, im ready." At that second, Yakima tapped lightly on the door. "Who's there?" grumbled old Frog. Yakima said nothing. The old man commenced and continued his talking to the Lord, when Yakima again knocked at the door.

"Who's there?" asked Frog, now agitated with a frown on his face and voice trembling. Still Yakima would not reply. Again Frog continued, and said, "O Lord, you know as well as I do that southern white folks are not prepared to go to heaven, but I am, when the angel of the Lord comes, I'm ready to go." Yakima knocked on the door again. "Who's there?" whispered Frog.

"The angel of the Lord," replied Yakima, in a somewhat soft and angelic voice.

"Why has the angel of the Lord come here?" asked Frog, as if he were much frightened.

"I've come for you!" replied Yakima, in the same angelic voice.

"Frog ain't here; he die three weeks ago," Yakima and his friend couldn't stop laughing when the old man answered. Frog hearing them, and realizing that the boys were playing with him, opened his door, came out with stick in hand, and said, "Is that you, Yakima? If I catch you, I'll teach you a lesson."

Yakima and his friend ran from the garden, laughing and joking, saying "the old man's not ready to visit the Lord, right now, as he wants everybody to believe."

CHAPTER 6

PAULET IN CHAINS AGAIN

Paulet was held in a cage behind the county jail. Her eyes glowed in the dark, her head browed, she slumped like a withering flower in the desert. She was caged. Caged like cattle. She was some-one's property! She was treated like livestock! She had been betrayed, and her daughter had been taken.

Windborne had sex with Paulet, and after having his way, he brought men with money to her cage who paid for a few minutes in privilege. They paid him a handsome dollar to enjoy the slave-trader's prize. Many who saw her were bought to tears at the pitiful sight, and were struck with wonder of her intelligence. When she spoke of her child, they realized that her heart was broken. The slave trader kept close watch over his property, because he feared that she might kill herself. There was no danger of that, because Paulette still hoped and believed that Kenneth would come to her rescue. She could not bring herself to believe that he would allow her to be sent away without seeing her, and the slave trader did everything he could to keep her thinking that.

Paulette, with a broken heart had sleepless nights thinking of her daughter. Kenneth's wife did everything within her power to make his life a pleasant and a happy one, Loretta was also in love with him. But guilt and shame sometime have unpredictable out-comes. He had not visited his mother-in-law since the evening he had given her permission to do whatever she wished to Paulette and Paula. He didn't want to go near the house, because he didn't want to see his dauther enslaved.

Loving, caring with a good heart, unlike her mother, she felt her husband's pain. She knew that some white men fell in love with slave-women, and she knew that he was one of the many; but she didn't want to let her mother know that she felt that way. Again and again she noticed the resemblance between Paula and Kenneth, she wanted the child to be sent away. Loretta was determined to mention the matter to her husband. The next morning, when they were sitting on the back porch, and the sun was pouring its splendid rays upon everything around, changing the leaves and hills in the distance into streaks red and gold, she asked. "Kenneth, what do you intend to do with Paula?" A paleness spread over his face, tears trickled down his cheeks. Suddenly the deep emotion that was visible in his face, when he tried to speak; his voice trimbled. Deep covered up emotion showed that she had touched a tender chord. Without a word, he buried his face in his handkerchief, hiding his tears.

This made Loretta still unhappy, because she feared that he had misunderstood her; and she immediately expressed her regret that she had mentioned the subject. Becoming satisfied from this that his wife sympathized with him in his unhappy situation, Kenneth told her of the agony that filled his soul, and Loretta agreed to intercede for him with her mother and have Paula sent to a boarding-school in a Free States. That afternoon, when Kenneth returned from his office, his wife met him with tearful eyes, and told him that her mother was filled with rage at the mention of the removal of Paula from her home.

The slave-trader, Windborne, was traveling South with his property. Paulette was to be a maid. Windborne had sold her to Mr. Burly Tomlin. Mrs. Tomlin was a severe mistress. Slaves who lived with her were well-dressed, poorly fed, and over-worked. Paulette found her new situation far different from her Virginia cabin-life. She had frequently heard Gloucester spoken of as a cruel place for slaves. A few days after her arrival, Mrs. Tomlin proved that she was anything but a pleasant and agreeable mistress.

Paulette was with her new mistress only a short time when she was ordered to cut her long hair short, and the sleeves of her dress altered to fit tight on her arms. Even with her hair short and with her altered dress, Paulette was still beautiful. Her life had been a secluded one, and though now twenty-eight years of age, her beauty had only been seen by few people.

"That mulatto "thought she was white when she came here, with that long curly hair of hers," replied Pam.

"Miss Tomlin made her cut that stuff off."

Paulette's radiant beauty was envied by most women, as well as by Mrs. Tomlin. She forced herself to remember that the house-servant lived better than other slaves. Even with her dreadful conditions, and harsh treatment Paulette experienced in her new home was nothing compared to the grief she endured, being separated from her child.

Refusing to eat, they feared she would die, and their money would be wasted, they decided to sell her. Paulette was sold at a private sale to a man to be his housekeeper. Mr. Cowpea, the new master, was a man of pleasure. He was the owner of a large sugar plantation, which he had left under the charge of an overseer. At first Mr. Cowpea tried to win her favor by flattery and gifts. Paulette dreaded every moment with him hoping that he would sell her again. At every sexual encounter with Cowpea she stated that she had left a husband in Virginia, and could never give herself freely to another man. He did what he wanted too anyway, by resisting; in her mind she was faithful, to Kenneth. The jewelry and clothing which Cowpea gave to her were rarely worn.

Alex like Paulette had been separated from his relatives. One day Paulette told him that her hair was growing out again.

"I can see," replied Alex; "you look like a man with short hair."

"I've been told that, if I had some money I'd runaway from this place." Seconds later, Paulette feared, she'd said too much, and laughingly observed, "I am always talking some nonsense, don't pay attention to me."

Alex was a tall, full-blooded African, from Senegal, his face revealed intelligence. Being a skilled worker, he had earned far more money than he had paid to his owner for his time, and this he had laid aside, with the hope that he might some day save enough to purchase his freedom. He had in his chest about two hundred and fifty dollars. He felt deeply for others, and he wiped the tears from his eyes while listening to Paulette's story.

"If she can get free with a little money, I'll give her what I have?" thought he, and as suddenly decided to do it.

An hour later, he entered Paulette's room, and, placed the money in her lap, and said...

"There, Miss Paulette, you said if you had the means you would leave this place. There is money enough to take you to Mexico, where you will be free. You are much fairer than most white women; you can easily pass for white."

At first Paulette thought it was a trick, but she was convinced by his manor of speech, that he was sincere.

"I'll take the money," she said, "on one condition, and that is if you come me."

"How?" he asked.

"I'll dress as a southern gentleman, and you'll pretend to be

45

my servant, and we will board a ship in Dover, and from there to Toronto."

With confidence in Paulette's judgment Alex accepted the proposition. The clothes were purchased; everything was arranged, and the next night, while Mr. Cowpea was on one of his drinking sprees, Paulette, under the assumed name of Mr. Barberry, with Alex in attendance as a servant, took passage from Dover in the ship *The Fantasy*. With a pair of wire-framed glasses over her eyes, in addition to other camouflage, Paulette made quite a gentlemanly appearance. To avoid conversation, she stayed in her state-room, pretending to be ill.

Meanwhile, Alex was playing his part as the servants. He bragged about his master's wealth, and his fine mansion. "I don't like these steamboats," he said. "I hope when Master goes on another journey, he'll take a carriage and the horses."

After ten days of traveling on an angry ocean, *The Fantasy* landed at Toronto, and Mr. Barberry and his servant walked on shore.

"Alex, you are now a free man, and can go anywhere you wish," said Paulette; "but I need to go to Virginia, and search of my daughter."

This announcement fell heavily upon Alex's ears, and with tears he begged her not to go; but Paulette had made up her mind to rescue Paula if possible.

Taking a boat for Norfolk, Paulette was soon on her way to her native State. Several months had passed since she left Cape Charles, and all her thoughts were on now on Paula. It was with a throbbing heart that she boarded a wagon on the Eastern Shores heading for Cape Charles.

It was late in the evening when the wagon arrived at Cape Charles; again Paulette was in her place of birth. She had intended to seek lodging on the outskirts of the town, but the lateness of the hour forced her to stay in a hotel for the night. She had scarcely entered the inn before she recognized a servant that she knew, she hoped her masquerade would keep her from being discovered. The desperate desire to free her child had made Paulette come to a place from which she had very little hope of escaping, to attempt to rescue her child. She was risking her own freedom for Paula's. She stayed in the hotel that night, and early the next morning, pretending that she was sick, breakfast was delivered to her room.

The next day, Paulet walked Along the Atlantic shore into the woods to see the cabin where she had spent so many happy hours. It was winter, the climbing plants and summer-flowers were not there. But there was that same path she had walked down many times, and the trees which had given her shade while she worked in her garden. Old memories pleasant and unpleasant surged through her mind and she began to cry. She was at home, near her daughter; but how could she find her? How could she see her? To do nothing she would have nothing to live for.

Three days passed, and Paulet returned to the hotel, she didn't have the slightest idea of where her child was. Unfortunately for Paulette, a riot had broken out among the slave population in Southampton Count, and all strangers were treated with suspicion.

The insurrection was headed by a slave name Nat Turner. He had felt the whip, and seen blood flowing from his body. He had witnessed the separation of his parents from their children; he knew slaves could expect no justice from the hands of slave-owner. He was a preacher, hated by white people, but loved and respected by blacks. On the discovery of the plan for the outbreak, Turner fled to the swamps, followed by those who had joined him in the in surrection. Turner was joined by a full-blooded Zulu, with a stern angry face.

47

Human Cattle

The marks on his face showed that he was from Africa. His clothing was made of skins of a wild bear.

Brought from the coast of Africa, at the age of twelve, to the island of Cuba, he was stolen from there and bought to Virginia. He had lived years in the swamps, and considered it his home. He had met a runaway slave woman, and, as they did in his native land, he rubbed her body with oils, performing a marriage ceremony. They had built a cave on a mound in the swamp, and this was their home. This man's name was Peculiar. His only weapon was a sword made from a piece of metal which he had stolen from a neighboring plantation. His dress, character, manners, and his mode of fighting were all in keeping with the earlier training he had received in the land of his birth, the Ivory Coast. He moved about with the speed of a cat, and neither the thickness of the trees nor the depth of the water could stop him. He had a violent restless spirit and, when fighting he was vicious, seeking revenge; he covered his hands with blood of the whites he killed. Hunger, thirst, and loss of sleep, he endured and never complained. He was angry.

Her Master had run an article announcing her escape in the Eastern Shores newspaper; the police were looking for her. It was on the third day after her arrival she was in her room when two oficers entered and told her that they were talking to all strangers. Trembling she handed the key of her trunk to the officers. To their surprise they found nothing but female apparel in the trunk, which raised their curiosity, and caused a further investigation that resulted in the arrest of Paulette. There she waited for many days, slapped around and beaten severely, never hearing a kind voice, alone, hopeless, isolated, she waited for the time to arrive when the chains would be placed on her arms and legs, and she would be taken back to her owner.

Liberty Dendron

The arrest of Paulet was announced in all the newspapers, but created little or no sensation. The slave owners were too engaged in putting down the revolt among other slaves; and, although all the odds were against the slaves, the whites found it wasn't that easy to contain this revolt. Every day brought news of fresh outbreaks. The revolt had spread from Southampton County into every city and county in Virginia. Without a second thought and without pity, whites killed all blacks found beyond the limits of their owners' plantations. The blacks, fought back, setting fires to mansions, and killed anyone who tried to escape from the blazing flames. Thus slaughter, bloodshed and butchery were added to the bloodbath, and the blood of whites also flowed. Killings! Killings! And more killing! Whites killing blacks' and blacks killing whites'. And when it was over...no graves were dug for blacks, their bodies became food for dogs and vultures; and their bones were left to bake in the sun, remained scattered about. This was the statement that whites made; you are my property, and my servants.

On receiving the news of the arrest of Paulette, Mr. Cowpea mailed the sheriff a letter asking him to sell her to the highest bidder. She was, sold to Bubba Nottingham a slave trader, who at once placed her in a cage. She saw slaves sold and taken to ships, and sent to some part of the Deep South; a place she was sentenced to go.

The day before the evening she was to be sent away, when the guard removed her chains from her feet and hands, Paulette leaped from her cage and ran past the jailer running for her life. A bridge not far from the prison, which crossed a wide stream that flowed into a river that flowed through a dark and dense forest. Running for her life she jumped into the river. Swimming with all her might she header towards the tree covered bank on the other side of the river. So unexpected was her escape that she swam across the river before the jailer or guard could lock the other runaway slaves in the jail or cages. It took them nearly an hour to organize a search party. During that hour she crossed the river and fled into a section of the woods that trees and vines were so thick that horses couldn't be used; fortunately for her bloodhounds were not available to run her down, she was moving fast.

The jailer and his search-party crossed the river and found her footprints. She was moving fast and staying in the thickest section of the woods, and skirting the outskirts of a huge plantation. Running... still running for her life now, with greater speed. After crossing the river with a greater distance between her and her pursuers now in-creasing, Paulette crossed another stream, she felt good. Her heart was pounding but she kept moving. She had nearly another mile to go and she had to cross another bridge; then she could hide in the woods. It was dark now and darkness was all around her, even the light of the moon couldn't penetrate the thick overhanging trees and vines. This was the woods she had played in as a child, that she new so well, would protect her from the pursuit of her enemies, tonight.

Still running for her life, as she approached the bridge, men on horse back formed a line across the narrow bridge to trap her. Seeing the escape was impossible, she stopped suddenly, and turned to fight her pursuers. On came the evil and angry white men faster than ever, already taking pride in her capture, and threatening punishment for her flight. For a moment she looked wildly and anxiously around for a path to escape. Far below, flowed deep violent waters. In-front and behind were sounds of approaching hooves of horses carrying men, shouting curse words. Realizing it was impossible to escape. She gripped the railings and jumped off the bridge, and sank beneath the angry foaming waters. The angry currents carried her miles away. The thrashing angry water under the cover of darkness, save her life.

50

That was when she decided to leave this country forever.

CHAPTER 7

THE MISTREATMENT OF PAULA

Seven years after Paulette had vanished. During that interval, Kenneth, finally realized that nothing could make Mrs. Cavalla give up her hold on Paula, and not willing to challenge her because of her wealth, he lost all interest in the child, and left her to her fate. Although Mrs. Cavalla treated Paula with a degree of harshness, still the child grew every day more beautiful, and her hair, though kept closely cut, seemed to have gotten softer, silk-like appearance. Now twelve years of age, and well-developed, Mrs. Cavalla began to love her.

Kenneth and Loretta had just returned from Washington, where Kenneth had several very important meeting as a member of Congress, and where he had lived for three years without returning home. It was on a beautiful evening, just at twilight, while seated at his living room window, He saw a young woman pass by and go into the kitchen. Not aware of ever having seen the person before, he went to see who the girl was. He met her in the hall as she was about to leave.

"Who have you come to see?" He asked.

"Miss Loretta," was the reply.

"Why do you want to see her?" he asked.

"My mistress told me to give her and Master Kenneth her compliments, and ask them to come over and spend the evening."

"Who is your mistress?" he eagerly inquired.

Human Cattle

"Mrs. Cavalla, sir," responded the woman.

"What's your name?" asked Kenneth, voice trembling.

"Paula, sir," was the reply.

The overwhelmed father stood completely amazed, looking and remembering, happier days, when he held her on his knee with so much love fondness and eagerness. It was then that he saw his own face and Paulette's features in herface. It was then that he was taken back to the days when with a woman's devotion, Paulette hung him and told him how lonely the hours were in his absence. He could control his feelings no longer. Tears flowed from his eyes. Turning abruptly, he walked into the living room.

When Loretta's return from her shopping tour, she found Kenneth in a downhearted mood. Loretta had borne him no children, and he loved his child, he told his wife that he was going to remove his daughter from the hands of her mother. When this news reached Mrs. Cavalla, through her daughter, she became furious with rage and called Paula into her room, stripped her shoulders bare and whipped her in thee presence of Loretta. It was nearly a week after Paula had been whipped, for no reason when her father was told by one of the servants. He went to Mrs. Cavalla and demanded his child, but it was too late...she was gone. To what place she had been sent no one would say, and Mrs. Cavalla refused to give any information.

It was a cool evening after a cloudless day, with the sun reflecting orange rays on the surrounding hills which were covered with a beautiful grassy area, and the flourishing greenness that gave the appearance of the tropics. The ship name Morning Glory drifted into the dock at Hicksville, and began unloading the cargo, taking in passengers and preparing to proceed on her voyage to Carolina. The plank connecting the boat with the shore had scarcely been secured in its place, when a man about fifty years of age, with a white neck-tie, and a pair of gold-rimmed glasses was boarding the ship.

"How do you do, sir, Mr. Hall, said, while taking from his mouth a large cigar, throwing it on the ship's deck."

"You have me at a disadvantage, sir," replied the man.

"You know me! My name is Windborne; I sold you a splendid beautiful black woman any years ago."

"Yes, yes," answered the man. "I remember you now, the woman died, and I never got the worth of my money out of her."

"I had no control of that," said the slave-trader;" she was healthy when I sold her to you."

"Oh, yes," replied the preacher, "I know she was; but now I want a young girl, fit for house use."

"I have one," said Windborne, "follow me," They walked to the stern of the boat to where the slave trader had nearly seventy slaves, most of them women.

"There," said Windborne. A beautiful woman sat on the floor.

"There, sir is the very gal that was made for you."

"That woman is white?" said the man.

"Oh, no, sir; she's not white!"

"Is she a slave?" asked the preacher.

"Yes," said the slave trader, "I bought her in Cape Charles, and she comes from an excellent family. She was raised by, Mrs. Geraldine Cavalla, one of the most self-righteous ladies I've ever known."

"She resembles in some respect Maggie, the woman I bought from you," said Mr. Hall. When he said the name of Maggie, the young woman stared as if she had been struck. Her pulse seemed to quicken, but her face alternately flushed and turned pale, and tears flowed from her eyes. It was a name she had heard her mother mention, and it brought to her memory those days...those happy days, when she was so loved and stroke in the deepest crevices of her memory.

Human Cattle

"Paula is the granddaughter of Maggie." The preacher, on learning the fact, purchased her, and took her home, feeling that his daughter Tonya would enjoy her company. Tonya treated Paula more like a sister than a slave, who, unknown to her father, she taught Paula how to read, and did much toward improving and refining Paula's manners, for her own sake. Like her mother she was fond of flowers, spent many of her leisure hours in the garden. Watching the flowers grow in the fertile soil...unplanted memories lingered in her mind.

In Tallahassee Paula found herself enjoying the fragrance of mangrove trees. She loved the pleasant scent of tropical flowers and chirping sounds of tropical birds. When she went with her young mistress to her friend's plantations, as she often did, Florida's wild richness greeted her, in Florida she felt at ease. The pleasant aroma of lime and orange trees, intertwining with the sent of hundreds of mango trees, with its ripe fruits, and water melons and cantaloupe's pungent aroma and the unblemished beauty of rows and rows of dark green vegetables, all welcomed Paula. When at the farm, Knox, the overseer, kept his eye on Paula because he knew she was a slave, and hoped that she might some day fall into his hands. Paula avoided him as she would of the fangs of a venomous snake.

The black overseer tried to insinuate himself into the good graces of Tonya and the company that she brought. Knowing that Miss Hall hated slavery, he was always trying to show that the slaves under his charge were happy and contented.

One day, when Tonya and her friends from Main were there, the overseer ordered the slaves to come to the "mansion,"and told the women to dance. After awhile whiskey was brought in and a small amount was given to each slave, in return, they were expected to give a toast, or sing; when it came to Kumquat's turn he said..."The big bee flies high, the little bee makes the honey: black folks do the work, and white folks gets all the money."

The overseer was not happy with Kumquat's toast. Mr. Hall had recently purchased Kato to assist around the house and to act as coachman. He was of pure west African blood, very dark, very handsome, tall, slim, and dignified. His bright brown eyes ligt up his face. His hair, hung in curls above his shoulders. He was brave and daring, strong in person, with intense emotions, yet kind and true in his affections, and earnest in his thoughts.

Paula had been at the preacher's house only a few weeks when Tonya noticed that closeness had grown between her and Kato. As time passed, they became more and more attached to each other. After satisfying herself that these two were in love. Tonya told them, they should get married, but Kato was planning to escape, and feared if he got married, it could influence his decision. Tonya taught Paulette and Kato how to read and write. Kato said that no master would ever whip him. Aware of his high spirit, Paula feared that an unforeseen problem might arise between Kato and Mr. Hall. One day Mr. Hall was angry because of Kato's lack of respect. He ordered Kato to follow him into the barn. Kato obeyed Mr. Hall but the servants knew that he would not submit to be whipped.

"No, sir," replied Kato, when Mr. Hall told him to take off his shirt: "I will serve you, Master Hall. I will labor for you day and night, if you ask me; but I will not let you whip me."

The preacher grabbed Kato by the throat and choked him; but he found his match. Kato knocked him down and beat him, and escaped through the back-yard running towards the woods. Recovering somewhat from the effect of his fall and beating, Mr. Hall struggled to his feet, pulled out his pistol, and started in pursuit of Kato. Finding, however, that Kato had runaway, he called for the dogs. Chuck was sent for, and in less than an hour, eight or ten men, including Mr. Hall, were in the woods with hounds, searching the trails.

The hunters were takeing bets on wether Kato will be taken dead or alive. The men had been in the woods a short time when the dogs hit the scent of two slaves, one was Kato. The slaves were heading for the swamp, with the hope that the dogs would be unable to follow their scent through the water. Nearer and nearer the whimpering, barking, howling dogs got; men were shouting, and cursing to let the escaping slave know that they were on histrail. All at once something flashed through the minds of the fleeing slaves. The scent became warmer and warmer, and what was at first an irregular whimper, became barks.

When the slaves reach the river, one of the slaves hid in the tall grass. Kato ran along the shore in the opposite direction of the slave hiding in the grass followed by the dogs. Kato was caught and and Kato was put in jail, and the other slave escapes.

Tonya tried to comford Paula, when they heard, through one of the slaves, that Mr. Hall had started with the dogs in pursuit of Kato. Paula knew that if he were caught, he would be severely punished, if not killed. It was with a greaving heart when Tonya heard the footsteps of Mr. Hall. The preacher shouted at his daughter angrily, telling her to ask no questions about the hunt. Tonya hoped that Kato wouldn't be caught; she wished it for the sake of the other slaves, especially for her maid, whom she regarded more as a companion than a servant. But the news of Kato's capture had spread through the mansion, and found its way to the ears of the weeping and heart-stricken Paula.

Mr. Hall had not been home more than an hour, when members of his church came calling, asking if they should take Kato from the jail and hang him. They were shouting in angry voices...no Blackman should be permitted to live after striking a white man; let us take him and hang him.

"The deacon is right," said another of the men; "if our slaves are allowed to challenge their masters...there will be no getting along with them."

"No, no," said Mr. Hall. "Let the law do our dirty work. As a Christian and God-fearing people, we'll let the law do our dirty work."

The men left. "This," said Mr. Hall, when left alone with his daughter. "This, has happened because of my kindness to those, black, savages. You have spoiled every one of them in this house. I can't whip any of them, without being in danger of having my life taken."

"I've done nothing to make a servants disobey your orders." Replied Tonya.

"Not intentional, my dear," said Mr. Hall, "But you're too kind to them. There's Paula. That girl walks around the house with as air...as if she's a mistress. Someday you'll be sorry."

"Paula is smarter than both of us; someday she will hold a higher position than that of a servant." Answered Tonya.

"You let her know that she was smart?"

The Saturday afternoon following, the capture of Kato, while Mr. Hall was in his study preparing for his Sundays service, Tonya entered the room and asked in an excited tone if it were true that Kato was to hanged next Thursday.

Her father told her that was the decision of the judge.

"Then," said Tonya, "Paula will die of grief."

"Why?" her father asked.

"She hasn't eaten, since he's been caught," replied Tonya.

"I'm preparing my sermon." While the man of God spoke, he

said. "Sometime we are forced to do the devils work."

Tonya tried to soothe Paula's feelings, she told her to put her trust in God. Unknown to her father, she allowed Paula to go to the jail every evening to see Kato, and during those visits, in spite of her own grief, Paula would try to comfort him with the hope that he'll live a better life in heaven.

Time passed, the day was approaching that Kato was to die. Hearing that some secret meeting had been held by the blacks, prior to Mr. Hall attempt of to whip Kato. The magistrate thought that Kato was the leader of the revolt. He beat Kato to get information from him, but the beatingt was in vain...

When questioned as to whether he knew of a conspiracy among the slaves against their masters, he replied...

"I wouldn't tell you if I knew?"

"If you know anything, and you tell me, I'll save your life!" said the magistrate

"My life is worth nothing." Stated Kato.

Everyone present was startled at the intelligence of which he had spoken.

"He's a very dangerous man," remarked one.

"Yes," said another, "he got some book-learning somewhere, and that's spoiled him."

An effort was made to learn from Kato where he had learned to read, Kato said nothing.

Paula entered the prison to see Kato for the last time. He was to die in the morning. Her face was covered with her hands, and tears were flowing down her face. With her heart pounding and hands trembling, trying to conceal her deepest emotion, she threw her arms around his neck and embraced him through the jail bars. Whispering in his ear, she told him, she had thought of a way to help him escape.

Heavy gray clouds hung over Tallahassee, and rain fell so hard it started to flood. The wind was gushing over a hundred miles per hour. It was a hurricane. Paula revealed to Kato her plan for his escape.

"Put on these ladies clothes," she said, "hurry while the cell door is open."

Kato resisted. He didn't want to leave her, but being convinced by Paula that her life would not be in danger, he decided to make the attempt. Paula being very tall, she thought no-one would notice, with the storm raging so violently. She took from her pocket a bunch of keys and unfastened the padlock, and unlocked the door to his cell.

"Come, girl, it's time for you to go," said the jailer.

Dressed in the clothes Paula bought him, Kato embraced Paula, and put his handkerchief to his face, and walked out of the jail.

Kato had barely passed the prison-gates, regretting having taken such a step. There seemed to him no hope to escape out of the State, he could excape for perhaps a few hours or days at most. By getting his freedom, the woman he loved had been sacrificed. He was thinking of returning, when he remembered Paula's words. "Be a man and stay strong. I have a plan!"

Paula had placed men's clothes in a leather sack, behind the jail where Kato could get them. Running towards the woods, Kato changed his close while heading towards the river. Traveling at night and sleeping during the day. His best way to escape would be by a boat, there were always ships anchored in Panama City. Thought. "If a ship is heading in any direction, I'll stowaway?" After traveling for days he reached the Mississippi where a ship was just coming in.

"Heading north," shouted the captain. As the passengers were boarding, Kato helped the slaves load bales of cotton. "Jump into the hold, and help them," said the mate to Kato, thinking that, he was working his way up the river. Once in the hull among the boxes, Kato hid. Many hours and days passed without water or food. More than once he started reveal himself; but knowing that he would be sent back to the plantation kept him from doing so. At last, with lips parched and fevered, Kato crawled out into the freight-room, and looked around. The hatches were locked, and the room dark. There were several bottles of wine and fruit. He opened a crate of bananas and helped himself. On the eighth day, the boat tied up at the wharf at the place of her destination. It was late at night; all but a man on watch was on shore. The hatches had been removed, and Kato quietly made his way on deck and jumped on shore. A man saw Kato, but it was too late to catch him.

Still in a slave state, Kato didn't know what to do. He didn't have any money to buy passage to Toronto. He ran, following the North Star, trying to follow the Ohio River, Kato soon found an opportunity to cross over into the State of Indiana. In Indiana he learned that some whites were the felt the same as those in slave states. And he learned, from other colored people that he met, that it was not safe to travel by daylight. While making his way one night, with nothing but the prospect of freedom, he was pounced upon by three men who were lying in wait for another runaway slave, an advertisement of whom they had received through the mail. Kato tried to tell them that he wasn't a slave. They had not caught the man they expected; but, if they could make him tell them where he had come from, they knew that a price would be paid for his capture.

Tortured by the slave-hunters, to make him reveal the name of his master and the plantation from whence he had escaped, Kato gave them a fictitious name in Virginia, and said that his master would pay a large reward, and pretended to be willing to return to the plantation. By this misrepresentation, he hoped to have another chance of getting away. Tempted with the prospect of a large sum of money, the slave-catchers started back with Kato. Stopping on the second night at an inn, on the banks of the Ohio River, the men, now tired and sleepy chained Kato to a bed-post in their room.

The men went to bed late, after an evening of drinking and celebrating. After midnight, when all was still, Kato arose from the floor, where he had been lying. Looking around he realized that the men were drunk. With a pounding heart and calm head he scanned the room. The door was locked, but the warm weather had forced them to leave the window open. If he could get his chains off, he could escape through the window. Their clothes were hung on a chair by the bed. Kato searched their pants pockets and found the key. The chains were soon off, he started for the window. He stopped, and said to himself, "I'll teach them a lesson?" He dressed himself in their best clothes, hung his old worn-out tattered clothes on the chair, and stepped out of the window, and climbed down one of the pillars, and headed north.

Dawn came before Kato found a hidingplace. The sun had just begun to rise when he turned and saw men coming on horseback. To the right was a farmhouse, men were asking if anyone had seen him. It was too late to turn back, the men that had captured him were behind him; and strange looking men were in front. The men on horses he knew were enemies, but he had no idea of what kind of men the farmers where. The farmers also saw the white men coming, and motioned for Kato to come. The broad-brimmed hats that the farmers wore told Kato that they were Quakers. Kato had seen some of these strange people while traveling, up the Missippi River, and had heard that they disliked slavery. He ran toward a farmer opening the barn-door, telling him to go in."

When Kato entered the barn, the farmers closed the door, and stood outside and confronted the men, who now came up demanding permission to enter, feeling that they had Kato trapped.

"Thee can't enter my premises," said one of the men, in a stern voice.

The men stated their claim to Kato, and said that, if they were not given permission to get him, they would force their way in. By this time, other Quakers gathered in front of the barn-door. Unfortunately for the slave hunters, and most for fortunately Kato, the farmer's friends had been holding a meeting in the neighborhood, and none of them had gone homes. After talking, the Quakers promised to let the slave hunters have Kato if they came back with a police officer, and a search-warrant. One of the men was left behind to make sure that Kato didn't get away, and the others went for a police officer. In the mean time, the owner of the barn locked the door.

After an hour searching for a policeman, they returned with an officer and a warrant. The Quaker's demanded to see the paper, and, after staring at it for some time, told his son to go into the house for his glasses. It took a long time for Aunt Lila to find the leather case, and when she did, the glasses needed to be cleaned before they could be used. After adjusting them on his nose, he read the warrant slowly.

"Mr. Bolding, we can't wait all day," said the policeman.

"Well, than thee read it for me?" asked the Quaker.

The officer complied, and the Quaker said. "Yes, thee may go in, now."

On approaching the door, the men found hundreds of huge nails in it.

"Give me your hammer and a chisel, if you please, Mr. Bolding," said the policeman.

"Please read that paper over again, will thee?" asked the Quaker. The policeman read the warrant again.

Liberty Dendron

"I see nothing there which says I must furnish thee with tools to open my door. If the want a hammer, thee must go elsewhere for it; I tell thee plainly, thee can't have mine."

The tools to open the door were gotten, and, after another hour, the slave-catchers are in the barn. Three hours is a long time for a slave to be in the hands of Quakers. The hay is tossed, and the barn is searched; but still Kato is not found. Brice has a smile upon his face. Dudley shakes his head knowing; little Mathew knew nothing, and, looking toward the house, Aunt Lila's smiling face, was announcing breakfast is ready.

"The nigger is not in this barn," said the policeman.

"I know he isn't," answered the Quaker.

"Why did you nail up your door, as if you were afraid we would enter?" asked a slave hunters.

"It's my door," said the Quaker.

Kato had gone in the front door and out the back; and the reading of the warrant, nailing up of the door, and other delay tactics of the Quaker, was to give him time to escape. It was now late in the morning, and the slave-catchers were a long way from home, and the horses were tired by the rapid manner in which they had traveled. The Friends, delighted, returned to their homes for breakfast. The policeman went home, and the slave catchers headed across the Ohio River, saying. "We'll catch another one."

CHAPTER 8

COME WITH ME

Now eighteen, Paula had changed quite a bit, a great contrast to the time when she lived with Mrs. Cavalla. Her tall and well-developed figure; her long, silky black hair, fell in curls down her neck; her bright, green eyes lighting up her tinted face, and teeth that most people envy, she was even more beautiful than before. At times, there was a radiant smile upon her face, which would have warmed the heart of a religious person. Such was the personal appearance of the woman who was now in prison, to save the life of another. Would she be hanged, or would she receive a different kind of punishment? These questions Paula did not ask herself. Plainspoken, and generous to a fault, she always thought of others, never of her own welfare.

The long stay of Paula caused uneasiness to Tonya, but she didn't tell her father, because he had said she couldn't go to the jail to see Kato. When the clock in the liven room struck eleven, Tonya called Travis, and sent him to the jail to look for Paula.

"She left around eight o'clock...after the storm started," was the jailer's answer to the slave's questions.

The return of Travis without having found Paula set off an alarm; she didn't know what to do. The hurricane had changed to a tropical storm. Thought. "Paula could be out there hurt or she could have runaway, or killed herself. That thought saddened Tonya's heart." Still, she waited till morning before breaking the news of Paula's absence to her father.

The jailer discovered, the next morning that his prisoner was white instead of black, and his first impression was that the change of complexion had taken place during the night, through fear of death. This assumption changed; when the mild, sweet voice that answered his questions, told him that she has taken Kato's place. When learning that Paula was in jail dressed in male clothing, Miss Hall immediately sent her ladies clothes to change into. The news of the heroic and daring deception of the slave-girl spread through Tallahassee.

"I will sell every nigger on this plantation," said Mr. Hall, at the breakfast-table, "I will sell all of them, and buy a new heard and whip them every day."

Tonya wept for the safety of Paula; she was glad that Kato had escaped. In vain they tried to obtain by threats from Paula, where Kato had gone when questioned, she replied. "I don't know, and if I did I wouldn't tell you. I don't care about what you do with me. Dogs can't track him; the hurricane has washed his scent away." She smiled. Her unwavering manners seemed to challenge them, and the gaze in her eyes dared them to lay their hands on her.

Seven days, Paula sat in a cage in front of the prison, to be gazed at by crowds of unfeeling white people, drawn there out of curiosity. The word came to her at last that the court had decided to spare her life, on condition that she should be whipped in public, sold, and sent out of the State within twenty-four hours. This order of the court she would have embraced, if she hadn't been so attached to, Tonya, her mistress.

"Sell her to some one whose kind," said Tonya to her father, as he was leaving the house.

"I'll sell her to the highest bidder," replied Mr. Hall. "Whoever buys her can do whatever he wants to too her."

Tears flowing down her face, Tonya paced, sat, and lay in her room, in the absence of her father she was openly affected by her emotions. For many months Tonya's health had been declining, and the slightest bit of trouble would make her sick for days. She wasn't able to endure the loss of her friend, whom she dearly loved. Cathy came in and told Tonya, Paula had been given seventy-five lashes on her bare back, Tonya fainted and fell on the floor. The servants sat her on the sofa, while Cathy went to get Mr. Hall.

Mr. Hall didn't know Tonya was so sick. A vane had ruptured. The physician who came to the plantation told him that she was dying. Her and since of justice and kindness. Her greatest characteristic, never hindered, Tonya in her hour of death. She had always been kind to the slaves, and because of that, they respected her. At her request, the servants were brought into her room, to say goodbye. There lay Tonya, pale and feeble, dying, surrounded by slaves. Some on their knees at her bedside...praying, and others standing, weeping.

Cathy said, "Death is an equalizer; it doesn't respect age, sex, wealth, nor kindness. Nothing can stop it from happening...when Mr. Death decides to come. Even the most beautiful flowers wither and dies. So, also, with man; our days are as uncertain as a passing breeze. One hour you glow and look healthy...but the next, you're like that withering flower. Then she was gone. A silence flowed over the house when she was gone! The sound of grief and mourning heard throughout the mansion.

When Paula heard the news of Tonya's death? The deep gashes of the cruel whip had drained her strength. She was laying face down on the floor in the cage for all to see. A slave trader had purchased her, but he had postponed her removal giving her time to recover.

It was a steamy Sunday in September, with clouds over head, rays of sun was scorching the earth. Paula stood at a window in Nottingham's slave-pen in Savannah Georgia, gasping for a breath of fresh air. The bells of churches were clanging, calling people to their places of worship. White people were rushing to the houses of prayer; some followed by slaves carrying their master's Bible; other's followed by servants holding their mistress' fan; and some holding umbrellas over their master's head to shield him from the scorching sun. The clinging of the bells called people to the churches, and drowned out haunting groans of slaves beings held in slave-pen.

The evening breeze gushed through the barred windows of the prison. The clock on the jails wall had just struck nine on Monday morning, when hundreds of perople were seen standing outside the gates and doors of the slave-pen. Here stood the same people that had gone to church on Sunday, shouting and singing religious songs. Their Bibles were not with them, they had left their bibles at home. Even their long and solemn religious faces were cast aside. They had come to the slave-market to make their purchases. Methodists were in search of their brethren. Baptists were looking for those that had been baptized, Presbyterians were willing to buy fellow-Christians, whether baptized or not. Everyone was looking for a slave.

"She's beautiful," muttered a woman looking for a servant. "I wish my daughter was that pretty,"

People were talking about, the "beautiful African woman." A tall young man with an Italian looking face, with a curling mustache, exhibiting the air of a gentleman, strolled by. His eyes were fixed on Paula, he stopped for a moment, than he walked away; but he returned. He watched the young woman wipe away her tears, as he turned he took out his handkerchief to wipe his eyes. Again he returned and this time Paula hid her face. She had heard that foreigners use female slaves as mistresses, and they made bad masters, she evaded his piercing gaze. Again he walked away and again returned. He took a last look and rushed away.

Having entered military school at the age of twelve, and being with Tomlin to Portugal, Antonio Vega had never been in love. He viewed all women from the same stand-point; he respected them for their virtues. And often spoke of their goodness; he never dreamed of marring anyone. But now Paula's beauty had overwhelmed him, her shy look and dazzling eyes had stolen his heart. He breathed with difficulty and felt a shortness of breath, his heart throbbed, he felt strange, and started trembling; but he didn't know what was wrong. He had fallen in-love, and it had taken only a glance. Vega blamed himself for not asking about the woman before he left the market that morning.

His stay in Savannah was short... because yellow fever was raging; he wanted to leave even earlier. The disease appeared in a form unusually severe and disgusting. Its victims were of healthy and weakest people. The disorder began in the brain with uncontrollable pain followed by a fever. Fiery veins streaked the eye, the face was inflamed and dyed of a dark dull red color; the ears from time to time rang in pain. Mucous and secretions flowed thick and freely, making it impossible to speak; before speaking they were witnessing death. When the violence of the disease approached the heart, the gums were blackened. Sleep broken, followed by seizure, or by freighting visions, that was worse than the in waking hours; when the victim sunk into fantasy land, figments of the imagination controlled the brain. Then came tranquility piece of mind, follower by calmness and composure of manners. People not sick were kept away from the infected, and the dead were thrown in ditches and burned. Plantations owners stopped slaves from working until the fever passed.

The clock struck three when Mr. Strickland entered his house, followed by Paula whom he had just purchased at the slave-sale. Paula looked around wildly as she passed through the hall to meet his wife. Mrs. Strickland was pleased with her servant's appearance, and congratulated her husband on his well thought-out choice.

Amazeing," said Mrs. Strickland, after Paula had gone into the kitchen, "she looks like Miss Brenda Verso."

"Indeed," replied the husband, "I thought that, the moment I saw her."

"I've never seen two people that look so much alike, than that girl and Brenda Verso's," continued Mrs. Strickland.

Dr. Verso, the purchaser of Jessica, the youngest child of Maggie, and sister to Paulet had been living in South Carolina on Liberty Street, near the Strickland's, for more than eight years, and the families were on very intimate terms. They visited each other frequently. Every one noticed Paula's close resemblance to Mrs. Verso, and especially to her eldest daughter. Indeed, two sisters could hardly have been more alike. The large, dark green eyes, black, curly hair, tall, shapely figure, and beautiful exotic faces.

The morning after Paula's arrival in her new home. Mrs. Strickland whispered something to her husband, now both of their eyes were following Paula as she passed through the room.

"She is far above the station of a slave," remarked the lady. "I saw her, last night removing some books, and staring at them as if she were reading; and she's as white as me. I am almost sorry you bought her."

At that moment the front door-bell rang, and Paula hurried through the room to answer it.

"Miss Verso," said the servant as she returned to her mistress' room.

"Ask her to come in," responded the mistress.

"Now, my dear," said Mrs. Strickland to her husband, "just look and see, if you do not notice a striking, resemblance between the of Brenda and Paula."

Human Cattle

Miss Brenda Verso entered the room just as Mrs. Strickland stopped speaking.

"Have you heard, the Paulsen's are sick with the fever?" Stated the young lady, after asking about the health of the Strickland's.

"No, I had not; I was hoping it wouldn't come to our street," replied Mrs. Strickland.

All this while Mr. and Mrs. Strickland were looking at the features of their visitor and Paula and even the two young women seemed to be conscious that they were in some way the objects of more than usual attention. Miss Verso had scarcely departed before Mrs. Strickland started asking Paula questions about her childhood, and after questioning her she knew that Paula and Mrs. Verso were relatives.

Every hour brought fresh news of the potency of the fever, the Strickland's were now preparing to leave town. Mr. Strickland couldn't go at once; he decided to let his wife go without him, accompanied by her new maid-servant. Just as Mrs. Strickland and Paula were stepping into the carriage, they were told that Dr. Verso had been stricken with the fast-spreading disease, and, he was dead.

It was a beautiful day, with a fine breeze for the time of year, that Mrs. Strickland and her servant found themselves in the cabin of the splendid new ship, bound from Carolina to Mobile. Every berth in the boat was occupied by persons fleeing from the contagious disease. Late in the afternoon, Paula was looking out of a rear window of the sitting-room; she was astonished to see a man standing near her, with his eyes fixed intently upon her. It was the tall young stranger whom she had seen in Savannah in the slave-market a few days ago. She walked away, but the hot cabin and her need of fresh air made her again return to the window. The young gentleman appeared, and walked to the end of the sitting room; and spoke to Paula in broken

English. This confirmed her previous thoughts that he was a foreigner, and she was happy that she hadn't fallen into his hands.

"I want to talk with you," said the stranger.

"What do you want?" she asked.

"I saw you in the slave-market last week, and regretted that I didn't speak to you then. I returned in the evening, but you were gone." he stated.

Paula looked angrily at the stranger, and started to walk away, but the quivering of his lips and the tone of his voice captured her attention.

"I was going to buy you, and free you, but I was too late," he said.

"Why do want to free me?" she asked.

"I had a sister, who died three years ago; you look so much like her. If didn't know she were dead...I would think you were her."

"I'm not your sister; why are you taking so much interest in me?"

"The love I had for my sister I have for you." he said.

Paula thought that the man was untrustworthy. And his confession of love, confirmed her thoughts. She turned away and walked away. Hours passed. Darkness drifted over the Atlantic Ocean, and the ocean slowly merged with the darkening sky. Paula sat on a bench by the window; watching people talked and play with each other. The Italian once more appeared near the window. She feared that her mistress would see her talking to a stranger, and be angry.

"Why do you want to talk with me?" she said, as he walked over and spoke to her.

"I want to purchase you and make you happy," he said.

"My mistress will not sell me." she replied.

"Then, if I can't buy you, when the ship reaches Mobile, runa way with me, and you'll be free." said he.

"I can't," said Paula; Walking away. The man placed a pieced of paper, in her hand.

After returning to her room, she unfolded the paper; it was a one hundred dollar bill. Her first impulse was to return the money to the man, after examining the money closely, she saw in faint pencil-marks, "This is from a man that loves you." She was going to give it to her mistress, she returned to the sitting-room and Mrs. Strickland was talking with some ladies; she didn't dare to interrupt her.

Again, Paula sat by the window, and again the man walked over. She took the money from her pocket giving it back to him; but he wouldn't take it, saying..."Keep it; you might need it...when I'm far away."

"I don't understand," said Paula.

"Would you rather be a slave than be free?" asked he.

"I want my freedom." she replied.

"If you want to be free, come with me. We'll be in Mobile in two hours, when the passengers are going on shore take my arm. Cover your face with a veil, you will not be noticed. We'll board the ship waiting in the dock for Italy. I promise, only if you wish... I'll marry you as soon as we arrive in Italy."

This solemn promise, gave Paula confidence in the man. She decided to go with him. "But then," thought she, "what will happen if I get caught? I would be forever ruined, and I would be sold, and in all probability I'll have to work the rest of my life on a cotton or sugar plantation." The promise of freedom outeighed the danger. Dressed in her best close, Paula waited with her heart filled with fear looking forward to the moment when she was to take a step that would change her life forever.

Ships from Mobile to Europe were about thirty miles down the

Atlantic. Some passengers were hurrying to shore, but a tall gentle-man with a lady at his side strolled leasurely down the plank, and stepped on the pier. They were Antonio Vega and Paula.

CHAPTER 9

WHAT A SURPRISE

The third day after his illness, unexpected by his wife and daughters. His body had scarcely been laid in the earth before they were facing new and unforeseen problems. By the laws of the Slave States, the children were the race and status of their mother. If the mother is free, the children are free; if a slave, the children are slaves. Being unacquainted with the Southern code, and no one knowing that Jessica was black, Dr. Verso hadn't given the subject a single thought. The woman whom he loved and considered his wife was still a slave. Now that he he died his wife and children, without the proper pa-pers, are property. If their secret were revealed his wife and children would be slaves. Dr. Verso was deeply engaged in speculation, and though generally considered wealthy was very much in debt.

After Dr. Verso died and was buried, Mr. James Verso, one of his brothers, went to Carolina to settle up the estate. On his arrival there, he was pleased with and felt proud of his nieces, and invited them to return with him to Minneapolis, never entering his mind...or in his faintest dreams, that his brother had married a slave, and that his widow and daughters would be claimed as such. The girls them-selves never knew that their mother had been a slave, and therefore knew nothing of the danger hanging over their heads.

Human Cattle

An inventory of the property of his brother was taken by Mr. Verso, and placed in the hands of the creditors. These preliminaries being arranged, the ladies, with their relative, decided to leave the city and lived for a few days on the banks of Lake Pirie, where they could enjoy much fresher air than in the city. As they were about to step on the buggy, an officer arrested the three women... saying they were slaves and part of the estate.

Mr. Verso was overwhelmed with horror at the idea of his nieces being claimed as slaves. He asked for time, to get the funds needed to save them from such a fate. He offered to mortgage his farm in Minneapolis for the amount of money the creditors would receive for his niece's. The creditors stated that they were extremely rare property, and would sell for far more than common slaves, and they must be sold at auction.

Their uncle James Verso was forced to give them up to the officers of the law. Brenda, the oldest of the girls, was very beautiful, and closely resembling her cousin Paula. Tracy, though not as tall as her sister, was a very beautiful girl, and both had all the accomplishments and manners that wealth and station could procure. Though only in her fifteen year Tracy had fallen in love with Swain LaFayette, a young man, a student that worked in her father's office. The feelings were mutual, Swain was eighteen, because of his age he had hidden his feelings from her parents.

The day of sale came, and Mr. Verso attended, with the hope that either the generosity of spirit of the creditors or a lean placed on his farm in Minneapolis might save his nieces from the fate that awaited them. But his hope was in vain. The feelings of all present seemed to be lost in the general wish to become the masters of his nieces, who stood trembling, ashamed, and weeping as the crowd gazed at them, or as the intended purchaser examined their bodies.

Neither the presence of their uncle or Lafayette could at all lessen the disrespect and language of the officers, or stop the hands of those who wish to examine the property that was offered for sale. After a fierce and brutal contest between the bidders, the girls were sold, one for two thousand three hundred, and the other for two thousand three hundred and fifty dollars.

When Jessica's daughters were sold, she killed herself, and their uncle with a heavy heart, started home to Minneapolis with no hope of ever seeing his nieces again. The administrator had found among Dr. Verso's papers the bill-of-sale of Jessica, which he reseaved when he purchased her. He had intended to free her.

Vega and Paula boarded the ship going to Italy. The ship "The Amazing Janice Byrd" waited for the crew to store cargo and receive the passengers. Antonio took Paula on board, and they stood on deck. Dawn was over the horizon, the next morning "The Amazing Janice Byrd" weighed anchor and turned her prow toward the sea. In the course of three hours, the ship, with outspread sails, was rapidly drifting from land. Everything appeared to be promising. The skies were beautiful and clear with puffy clouds, and the sea calm. Around noon time clouds began to chase each other through the heavens, and the sea became rough. It was then that Paula felt that there was hoped of escaping. She had stayed in the cabin, but now she said that she wanted to go on deck. The puffy clouds were now over the horizon, they were dark and gray and drifting towards the rising sun.

As Paula came on deck, she strained her eyes trying to catch the final view of her native land. With a smile on her face, and her eyes filled with tears, she said…."Goodbye, I don't care where I go, 'as long as it is far from here."

Antonio Vega stood by her side, proud of his future wife, with his face glowing, as the wind rushed through glossy his black hair. *Paula whispered in his ear...*

"America is no longer home for me."

The winds increased with nightfall, and gloom beyond understanding surrounded the ship. The gloom was frightening. The attention which Antonio Vega paid to Paula, although she had been registered on the ship's passenger list as his sister, attracted unwanted attention because of the way they were acting, it was clear to all that she was more than a traveling companion. His tall, slender figure and handsome face bespoke for him at first sight. He was in love with Paula and all could see. The weather became even more turbulent as wind rushed over violent waves, making the ship crack and squeak. Nothing could be seen but violently thrashing water.

Day came and passed and the storm got even stronger. Misery hopelessness and anguish was now on every face. Bright flashes of lightning surged through dark gray clouds illuminated black angry waves that surrounded the ship, which was now moving swiftly, sailing sales flapping through gusting winds blowing from behind. After days of stormy weather, the Atlantic settled down into a dead calm, and the passengers flocked on deck. The last three days of the storm, Paula was so sick she could barely raise her head. Her pale face and quivering lips made her look as if she was dying. Her brilliant eyes, surrounded with lashes as dark as night, gave her an angelic appearance.

Paula had to have someone on which to focus her affections, she had lost all hope of ever seeing Kato. At first she respected Vega for the love he showed for her and for his willingness to sacrifice everything to free her. On this adventure she had risked everthing, if her heart were broken while fleeing for her freedom; she would still be free. Each day became more pleasant as the ship surged through heavy fog. The wind whistling as the breeze lessen bought comfort to their ear, and brought happiness and pleasure to the heart of every one on board. At last, the long nervousness was broken when they spotted land, the passengers leaped with joy. It was a sunny morning in October. The sun had risen, and sky and earth were still bathed in his greeting dawn, when the Amazing Janice Byrd entered the Mediterranean Sea and dock at Naples. The cobblestone streets, huge stone bridges, and smiling faces of the people. They had traveled more than thirty days across the Atlantic Ocean and Mediterranean Sea.

After getting their baggage cleared from the custom-house and going to a hotel, Antonio made immediate arrangements for their marriage. Paula, on arriving at the church where the ceremony was to take place, was overwhelmed at the sight. She had never seen a church so gorgeous as this. The clothing of the priest and people singing. The deep and solemn voices. The elevated crucifix. Carriages drawn by horses. The marvelously decorated altar and sweet-smelling incense; made this a dream that had come true. At the conclusion of the ceremony, the loud and solemn tolling of the organ's playing songs of praise were barely heard in the rear of the Catholic Church.

The happy couple set out at once for *Riviera di Vega*, the home of Antonio's parents. But their stay there was short, they had scarcely visited any of his friends when orders came for him to go to Portugal to join his military platoon, his platoon was stationed there. Not long after his arrival in Portugal, they left for India, passing through Spain and stopping in Lisbon, and back to Italy. In Italy, they spent a week, where Antonio introduced his wife to his brother officers. There the newly-married couple was introduced to Alonzo Kapolei, a very important man in Italy. When meeting such an important man, Paula acted like a proper lady.

Leaving Italy for Lisbon, they visited a huge factory. Three days later the took a ship from Rome to Algeria. The weather was very hot.

Human Cattle

On arriving in North Africa, Captain Vega and wife were received with honors...for his heroic bravery in several bloody battles. A Paula was complimented by all...all speaking of her exotic mesmerizing beauty and good manners, and the fact that she was married to man that everyone liked and admired didn't hurt. This was indeed a great change for Paula. Six months had barely passed since she was sold as a slave in the slave-market of Carolina. And now she was free.

Riding on a fast horse, with the Quaker's son for a guide, Kato pressed forward while Brice was deceiving the slave-catchers at the barn-door, through which he had just escaped. When out of danger, fearing that he might be stopped again if he continued on the road in open day, Kato hid in the woods until nightfall. With a broken heart, he watched the setting sun lingerer above the hills fade away. Alone, with nothing but hope of safety, he pushed forward for several nights. The new clothes he had taken from the slave traders, and the thirty dollars the young Quaker had given him, helped him in his flight toward freedom.

It was late in the evening when Kato arrived at a small town on the banks of Lake Erie, where he decided to stay that night. Strange were his feelings, in Canada he would be free and safe, not a slave. Nor would he ever feel the whip of a plantation owner, but his thoughts were with Paula. Was she still in prison, and if so, what was her punishment for helping him escape? Would he see her again? These thoughts haunted him while he slept; and awakened him from his sleep.

The alarm of fire aroused the roomers in the hotel in which Kato had sought shelter for the night. The whole village was buried. The wind was high, and the burning embers were carried on the breeze through the sky. The whole town was lighted up, women and children were crying in the streets. Kato heard the alarm and hastily dressed himself and rushed toward the burning building.

"Up there in that room on the second story, is my child!" shouted a woman, wringing her hands, asking someone to rescue her child. The fire was heading in the direction of the room in which the child was sleeping. All hope of saveing the Childs life was gone. The wind lifted the stream of smoke, revealing that everything was not lost.

A long ladder was brought and one end placed under the window of the room. A man mounted the ladder and climbed to the window. The smoke met him as he raised the window, and he cried out, "All is lost!" He returned to the ground without entering the room. Another man shouted. "The fire hasn't made it's to that part of the building." The mother, thinking that all hope was gone, raised her hands with grief. Minutes later, a man was climbing the ladder. All eyes looked up at the stranger as he vanished in a cloud of smoke. Cheers broke the stillness that had fallen on the crowd. Then the man was seen climbing back through the window holding under his arm a child. Another cheer and then another, the child had been saved. The man fainted at the foot of the ladder. The man was Kato. As soon as he was revived, he vanished, fearing that they would take from him his freedom.

The next day, Kato took a ship, and the following morning found himself standing on the soil of Toronto. As his foot touched the shore, he dropped to his kneed and kissed the earth. Paula occupied his thoughts even more now that he was free. He met, on his arrival in Toronto, other slaves who had escaped from Southern States; he rarely mingled with other people. The soft, silverorange tints on the leaves of the trees, with snow-spotted trunks, and a fidget air, welcomed and warned Kato that he was in another climate. He looked for work, and found it; and after working for months decided to return to America to search for Paula. The Frenchman, for whom he was working, offered to go south to purchase Paula, if she could be bought.

Three months passed, from the time Kato had started working for Mr. Maddox, when he returned from the South, and told Kato that Preacher Hall had sold Paula, and that she had been sent to the South Carolina slave-market. This news was so upsetting to Kato, he had left America forever. He had seen many of his friends die in his very presence, and he had seen his mother sold to the slave-trader. His sister had been sold like cattle; he had been sold and resold, and been forced to submit to the most degrading and humiliating insults; and now that the woman upon whom he had given his heart, without her his life was a burden, had been taken away forever, because of that, he hated Americans.

He loved his new country Canada. Listening to former slaves tell their stories, made him hate slavery even more. A woman told him how she had escaped from the south to be with her husband. They hadn't seen each other for years; still they rushed into each others arms. Some told storier of how their sister's were used to satisfy the master's needs. There were stories of a husband being whipped to death trying to protect his wife. He sat in the little log-cabin, by the fireside, and heard tales that caused his heart to bleed; he got angry because he knew that there was no reason for such unnecessary hate. It was with such emotion he told Mr. Maddox that he was leaving in three weeks.

Late in the month of February, Kato boarded a ship loaded with lumber, heading for Europe. The ship, though an old one was sound and seaworthy. Kato was working his way across the ocean. As the ship left Canadian waters and entered American waters, he was happy that he was leaving a country in which his right to manhood had been denied him, and his happiness destroyed. The ocean was swelling and the wind gushing. The little ship pushed its way through the thrashing waves, with American territory fast receding in the distance, Kato mounted a pile of lumber to take a last farewell with teary eyes, and quivering lips, he gaze toward America, and said..."With all your faults, I love you still."

Rain was falling on the dirty pavements of London as Kato walked off of the ship. Passing the custom-house, he took a buggy to Queen Ann Hotel on Ann Hill. Finding no employment in London, Kato decided to go further into the interior to look for work. He paid his bill and left London.

In Bedford, hotels charged more than he expected. After eating and paying his bill, and preparing to leave; a servant bowed, and said..."Something for the waiter, sir?"

"I paid my bill," replied.

"I'm the waiter, sir; my wages are what guest gives me."

Taking from his nearly empty wallet, Kato handed the man a half-crown; he was preparing to put it back into his pocket, and spotted another man waiting.

"What do you want?" he asked.

"Whatever you wish, sir. I am the other waiter."

The wallet was again taken from his pocket and another half-crown handed out. Stepping out into the hall, he saw standing there a woman, in a white apron.

"What is your job?" he inquired.

"I'm the chambermaid, sir."

Out came the wallet again, and he gave another half-crown; than another girl, with a fascinating smile, stood where the woman who had just received her fee.

Human Cattle

"What do you want?" asked Kato angrily.

"Sir, I am the other chambermaid."

Finding it easier to give shillings than half-crowns, Kato handed the woman a shilling, and again placed his wallet into his pocket, glad that another woman was not to be seen.

Preparing to leave again, three men walked over to him, one after another.

"What have *you* done?" he asked the first.

"I shined your boots, sir."

The wallet was taken out again, and a shilling was placed in the servant's hand.

"What do I owe you?" he asked the second.

"I took your letter to the post office, yesterday, sir," another shilling was given.

"In God's name, what have you done?" demanded Kato, now entirely out of patience.

"I told you the time this morning."

"Well!" exclaimed the indignant man, "you asked and you have to pay for my services."

He paid this last demand with a sixpence, regretting that he had not paid with sixpences instead of half-crowns.

Having cleared off all demands in the house, he started for the railway station; before he reached the street, he was approached by an old man with a broom in his hand, who, with a very low bow, said...."I work here, sir."

"I didn't send for you; what do you want?" asked Kato.

"I am the man that opened your carriage-door, when you came last Monday, and I know you won't allow a poor man to starve."

Putting a sixpence in the old man's hand, Kato once more

started to leave. Having gotten letters of introduction to persons in Bolton, he found no difficulty in getting a job in a large manufacturing house. Although the salary was small, the job was a much better one than he had hoped to get. His salary as an out-door clerk enabled him to employ a man to teach him at night, and, by studing and hard work, he was soon promoted.

After three years in his new home, Kato was placed in a higher position, where his salary amounted to five hundred dollars a year. Drinking, smoking, and other expensive habits, which clerks usually indulged in, he avoided. Being fond of poetry, his leisure time was spent reading books. The knowledge which he picked up during his hours of leisure gave him a great advantage over the other clerks, and in time his employers respected him far more than any other in their employment. So eager was he to improve himself...he read nights and morning before he started work, in this new country, his success was far beyond his expectations.

CHAPTER 10
LEAVING HIS NEW COUNTRY

Now in poor health, after ten years of working this job, Kato decided to give it up, and for a lest stressful job. It was on a foggy morning in the summer that he started for Dublin, having made up his mind to travel for his health. After visiting Downpatrick and Belfast, he decided to spend a few days in the old town of Londonderry, with a friend whose acquaintance he had made in Crookston.

During the second day of his stay in Londonderry, crossing the main street, Kato saw a carriage coming toward him with great speed. A lady was the only occupant in the carriage, and she was using all her strength to stop the frightened horses. The driver leaped from the carriage, and was following on foot with the crowd. Courage was one of his best characteristics. Kato leaped in front of the horses to stop them; grabbing the bit of the high-spirited animals as they dashed pass him. He was dragged several yards before their speed was reduced, which didn't happen until one of the horses stumbled and fell to the ground, Injuring Kato...struggling beneath him.

All present were convinced that this daring act had saved the woman's life, the horse-drawn carriage would have been ripped too pieces if the horses hadn't been stopped. On the morning following this very dangerous adventure, Col. Cunningham, visited Kato's residence, and, after expressing his admiration for his noble daring, and thanking him for having saved his daughter's life, invited him to visit him at his country residence. This invitation was promptly accepted in the spirit in which it was given; and three days after, Kato went to visit Mr. Cunningham. The house was surrounded by trees, and a stream in the rear, beds of flowers cast their sweet fragrance into the air. It was a pleasant place to spend the warm weather, the colonel and his family gave Kato a most cordial welcome. Miss Cunningham rendered special and unusual attention to their guest. He had not planned on staying longer than a few hours: but the family insisted on his taking part in a fox-hunt that was in the morning of the third day. He decided to stay.

Twenty men and five women; all were on the ground at the appointed hour. Miss Cunningham was, one of the women. Kato tried to excuse himself from joining in the chase. His plea of ill-health was only met by smiles from young ladies, and all said that a ride in the country would cure his illness. Dressed in a scarlet coat and high boots, with a round cap worn in the chase, Kato mounted a high-spirited horse, whip in hand, and rode with the others in the party. In America, riding is a necessity; in England, it is a pleasure. Kato wasn't a very good rider. He hadn't been on horseback for more than ten years, and as soon as he mounted, every one realized that he was a beginner, and smiles were on the faces of everyone.

The blowing of the horn and assembling of the hounds, and the release of the fox from his cage; was the signals for the chase to begin. The first half-mile the fox dashed over a grassy field where there wasn't a hedge or ditch. Thus far the chase was enjoyed by all, even by Kato, who would have rather watched the scene from a distance.

The first mile of the pursuit, was over smooth meadow-land, it had an exhilarating effect upon Kato's mind, but he wasn't in his element. He remembered slaves being chased by dogs in America. He hoped the fox had started for the dense forest which lay just in front them; he saw high walls and fences in that direction which appeared impossible to leap.

Up and away went the other hunters leaping over stone walls, high fences, and deep ditches. They leaped over fences, four or five feet high; all were quite at home in the saddle. All but Kato! He approached the first fence, and was about to make the leap, he pulled at the bridle, and shouted at the top of his voice, "Stop! Stop! Whoa!" the horse at the same time prancing about, and determined to keep up with the other horses. Leaped the fence, following the hounds, and all were soon lost to the view of Kato. Kato rode up and down the field looking for a gate or bars that he might get through without leaping another fence. Knowing that it was impossible to catch up with the others in the party, he returned to the house, pretending he was ill.

"Has something happened to you?" asked the groom.

Human Cattle

"Just a little dizzy," Kato answered.

One of the servants, without being ordered, went for the family physician. Ashamed to say that his return was because of his inability to ride, Kato pretended thst he was sick. The doctor came, felt his pulse, examined his tongue, and pronounced him a sick man. He immediately ordered a lukewarm bath, and sent for a couple of leeches. Seeing things taking such a serious turn, Kato regretted the lie he'd told; there was no fun in being rubbed and leeched when you were in perfect health. He had gone too far to turn back. He submitted quietly to the orders of the doctor; and, after following the orders given by the physician, was put to bed.

Shortly after, the sound of the horns and the barking and howling of the hounds; a servant announced that the fox had taken the back track, and was somewhere near the house. Even the pleasure of watching the hunt from the window was denied to Kato; the physician had ordered that he must stay in bed. At last the chase was over, and the hunters returned. After ten days of sweating, blistering, and leeching, Kato left his bed, with much reduced in flesh and strength. This was his first and last attempt to hunt a fox or follow hounds.

During his stay at Colonel Cunningham's, Kato spent most of his time in the library. No man read books with more interest than he. He read books about trees, grass, and water, to learn from nature. He searched books for knowledge of which he had been denied as a slave. After a few days spent in the highlands of Dublin, Kato passed hastily through London on his way to the continent. It was toward sunset on a warm day in October, shortly after his arrival in Italy, that, after strolling some distance from the Hotel the Cadenza, in the old and picturesque town of Cadenza, he entered a burial-ground. He enjoyed the silence. Grave yards were his favorite places. He loved *looking at fancy headstones of the dead.*

The silence was part of the sadness that hung over the resting-place of the dead. Even the birds respected the spirit of this place, because they were silent when flying over graves and playing without sound in the tall grass. After reading the various inscriptions that told mostly lies about the deceased, he stopped at a secluded spot where weeping willow branches bent so low they nearly touched the ground, it looked like they were hiding graves under them.

Kato was sitting on a tombstone reading a book. It was approaching dust, he had been reading only a few minutes when he saw a lady coming up the path, holding a boy, about five or six years old. A veil was covering her face. When she saw Kato she screamed and fainted. Kato sprang from his seat and caught her before she touched the ground. At that moment an elderly gentleman rushed over, which seemed to indicate that he was with the lady. The old man came up, in rather a concerned manner and asked what had happened, and Kato told him what he had seen. After picking up a small bottle, which had fallen from her hand, and holding the bottle a short time to her face, the lady began to revive. During all this time, the veil still covered her face. When she recovered, she frantically look around and raised her head slightly, and screamed again. The old man now thinking that Kato's dark complexion was the cause of the tragedy, said in a somewhat irritable tone. "It would be better, sir, if you leave us alone."

The little boy at this juncture started crying, and pointed at Kato, Kato left the cemetery and returned to his hotel. While seated at the window of his room looking out at the crowded street, every now and then he thought about that strange encounter in the graveyard with the woman. He remembered he'had left his book on the tombstone, and he decided to return for it at once. After a walk of nearly twenty minutes, he entered the cemetery and approached the spot where he had been. The moon was above, and its soft bright light danced above the pond. Kato searched for his book, it was nowhere to be found. There was nothing, but the bouquet that the lady had dropped, which layed half-buried in the grass. The stillness of death reigned over the place; and the birds that he had seen earlier, had retired for the night.

Lifting the bunch of flowers, Kato started for the hotel. "What does this mean? Why have they taken my book?" He asked himself. These questions he asked himself again and again as he walked. His sleep was broken more than once that night, and he welcomed dawn as it made its appearance. After a sleepless night, hearing the clock strike six, Kato took from his table a book, and decided to read a little before breakfast. While deeply engaged, a servant entered and handed him a note. Hastily opening it, Kato read as follows: Sir, I owe you an apology for the abrupt manner in which I addressed you last evening, and the inconvenience of which you were subjected. If you will honor us with your presence to-day at four o'clock, I would like to apologize in person. My servant will be waiting outside your hotel with a carriage at half-past three. I am, sir, Mr. Tuscola Vega. Thank you for you patience and assistance, Mr. Kato Amid.

Who is this gentleman, and how had he found out Kato's name and the hotel that he was staying in, was a mystery to Kato. And this note seemed to challenge him. He didn't know the stranger but he decided to accept the invitation. The clock on a neighboring church struck three when a servant announced to Kato that a carriage had come for him. In a few minutes, he was seated in a luxurious carriage drawn by a pair of the most beautiful black stallions, rolling over a cobblestone road shaded by trees. The carriage stopped at a beautiful villa.

Liberty Dendron

Kato stepped down from the carriage to the ground, and was escorted to a room, with finely decorated walls and splendid tapestry, on the ceiling. The walls were covered with fine oil paintings from the hands of great Italian masters, and one by a Chinese artist, of a monkish legend connected with the "Holy Church," and a painting of a beautiful lady. High-backed chairs were placed around the room, expensive curtains with African patterns were woven into its folds on both sides of the window, and a beautiful, very expensive, oriental carpet covered the floor. In the center of the room stood a table covered with books, in the midst of which was a vase of fresh flowers, filling the room with their various scents. A faint single candle glowed, accenting the quiet of the moment, gave beauty beyond description to the whole room. A half-opendoor cast a dim light on a marble floor to an adjoining room, with pictures, statues, and antiquated sofas, and flower-pots filled with rare plants of every kind and description.

Kato had barely scanned the room when the elderly man whom he met yesterday came into the room, followed by the little boy; the man introduced himself as Mr. Vega. A few minutes later a woman, a beautiful woman, dressed in black, with long black curly hair hanging over her shoulders, entered the room. Her dark, bright eyes got teary when she saw Kato. Mr. Vega immediately arose on the entrance of the woman, and Mr. Vega was about to introduce Kato when he noticed that Kato sat down on the sofa, in a faint voice saying…"It's you!"

After this, all was dark and dreary. How long he remained in this condition, it was for others to tell. The lady knelt by his side and wept; and when he came to, he found himself stretched upon the sofa with his boots off and his feet resting on a pillow. By his side sat Mr. Vega, with the smelling-bottle in one hand and a glass of water in the other, and the boy was standing at the foot of the sofa.

Human Cattle

As soon as Kato completely recovered and able to speak, he said..."Where am I and what does all this mean?"

"Take it easy...I will tell you." Replied Mr. Vega.

After the lapse of nearly ten minutes, Kato arose from the sofa, adjusted his apparel, and said, "I am ready to listen to anything you have to say."

"You lived in America?" said Mr. Vega.

"I did," Kato replied.

"You knew a woman named Paula," continued the man.

"I loved her."

"The woman you helped yesterday is she," said Mr. Vega.

Kato was silent, the mingled grief and joy made tears... flow from his eyes. Paula entered the room.

"How did you find out my name and address?" asked Kato.

"After you left the cemetery," replied Paula, "my boy said, 'Mum! He left his book!' I opened the book, and saw your name written in it and also found a card of the Hotel the Cadenza.

"Are you married?" asked Paula, with a pounding heart and trembling voice.

"Never, came close once," Kato's reply.

"Thank God!" she exclaimed.

It was then that hope gleamed in her face and she smiled.

"Are you single now?" asked Kato.

"Yes," she answered.

"Then you are mine." he said with a smile.

Her hair hung over her shoulders, and her Eyes full of life. Her pleasan sounding voice, made her appear even lovelier. Watching the two of them made Mr. Vega think of the time when he was young and his wife was alive.

Furnished by nature with willingness to study, and a memory

so good that all who knew her were surprised at the ease with which she acquired her education, Paula became an accomplished lady. After her marriage with Antonio, they moved to North Africa, where her husband's regiment was stationed. But soon after their arrival, a battle was fought with the natives, in which several officers were killed; among them was Captain Antonio Vega. There at the same time, her husbands father General Tuscola Vega, took care of her. And brought her back to Italy with him to his home. Mr. Vega had accumulated a large fortune, all of which would be left to his daughter-in-law and his grandson.

Although Paula had married Antonio Vega, she had not forgotten Kato, and her father-in-law willingly give his consent for her to marry him. And Kato still loved and desired her, even at this stage of his life. Her love would be enough for him. Paula knew he still loved her because he had never gotten married. His love was—a rare kind of devotion. She eagerly appreciated his proposal.

It was late in the evening when Kato led Paula to the window.The moonlight cast a shadow on their faces. This was the first evening that Kato had been with her since the night she had helped him escape. How different they were now. Free instead of slaves.

CHAPTER 11

THE HONEYMOON

It was Thanksgiving Day, when Kato and Paula set out for the Catholic Church, where the marriage ceremony was to be performed. The clear, chilly windy, frosty air mingled with cheerful optimum to every movement. The sun reflected off the stained windows, as Kato and Paula entered the church, followed by Mr. Vega. As the ceremonies came to an end, the priest gave his blessing to the newly-married pair, Paula whispered in Kato's ear. "No one will ever separate us again, I love you."

A smile was on every face as the wedding-party left the church and entered their carriage. It was a happy day, after so many years' of separation. Everything had been arranged for a honeymoon up the Mediterranean, to the Atlantic, and to the Caribbean Sea. The party set out the same day for South America. Floating down the Caribbean Sea they saw islands and rivers like they had never seen before, some were so thick with vegetation that a large ship could never reach its banks.

Their first docking-place for any length of time was in Venezuela, the most interesting place on the river. From Venezuela they went to Cuba, where they had the greatest attention paid them. Besides being provided with letters of introduction, Kato's very dark complexion created more attention than usually awarded to most wealthy travelers. Kato, with Paula, next visited the island of Hispaniola, the dirtiest city on the in the Caribbean Sea. This Catholic Church was larger and prettier than most churches in Europe. Kato and Paula looked up at the beautiful arches and columns of this breathtaking Church. Kato commented about its majesty presence surrounding it: There were villas, cottages, and huge mansions, and the enchanting winds of the Caribbean Sea gushed through the vine and fruit-covered hills.

After traveling miles and miles, they went to Jamaica. They had been given a letter of introduction to Alexander Lopez, a friend of Mr. Vega. They were invited to make his house their home during their stay. Ingering clouds exploded, and rain fell in streams. Kato and

Paula retired for the night. The sound of thunder, and flashes of lightening, leaped from valley to valley.

"I whish we were home," said Paula, as she heard groans coming from an adjoining room. The sounds, at first faint, grew louder and louder, indicating that someone was suffering; in extreme pain.

"I didn't like this hotel, when we came in," said Kato, relighting the lamp, which had gone out.

"Nor did I," replied Paula.

The shrieks increased, and then a scream... "She's dead! I killed her!

The thunder grew louder, and flashes of lightening more vivid, while the noise from the adjoining room increased.

Kato opened the door, to ask if he could help, he heard the words, "She's dead! She's dead! I didn't kill her, she's my child...my daughter. I loved her, and yet I didn't protect her."

"Whoever he is..." said Kato.

The storm continued to rage, and the loud sound of thunder and violent flashes of lightening, mingled with the shrieks and moans of the freighting cries in the adjoining room, made the night a fearful one. The long hours wore slowly away, but neither Kato nor Paula could sleep, and they arose at an early hour in the morning, ordered breakfast, and resolved to return to the house on the hill.

"I'm sorry, sir, that you were disturbed by the sick man last night," said the clerk, handing Kato his bill.

"I wish he would leave. Several people have left my hotel because of him."

"Where is he from?" asked Kato. "He's from the United States, and has been here nine days, and has been acting crazy ever since."

"Has he no friends with him?" asked Kato.

"No, he's alone," reply the clerk.

Human Cattle

Kato told Paula what he learned from the clerk, listening to him talk about the sick man, she asked him to find out what the man's name is. He went to the lobby and looked in the guest book, and, to his great surprise, found that the American's name was Kenneth Oar, from Cape Charles, Virginia. It was with feelings of extreme tenseness that Paula listened, to the words flowing from the lips of her husband.

"We must help him,"

"Who is he," Paula asked.

The desk-clerk was glad to hear that someone wanted to help the sick man. The clock in the hall had just struck ten, when Kato entered Kenneth Oar's room. Stretched upon unsheathed a mattress, with both hands tightly holding each side of the bed, Kenneth Oar was a pitiful sight. His receding hair had turned gray, he had a long unshaven beard, and wildness in his eyes. He looked at them strangely as they opened the door and entered. The faint hope which had so suddenly raised in Paula's heart, sink, and she felt that this man couldn't be kind to her. He had no resemblance to the man who was her father.

"Help me!" cried Kenneth Oar, as Kato and Paula walked into the room. His eyes glassy and voice shrieked and broke when words flowed from his cracked and fevered lips.

"No, I didn't kill my daughter! I didn't! She's not dead! She's dead...but I didn't kill her...poor girl! It is she! No, it cannot be! She can't come in here...you cannot be my Paula."

At the sound of her name, coming from the madman's lips, Paula gasped for breath, Kato noticed that she had grown pale. It was evident to him that her father was either guilty of some terrible act. His eyeballs rolled in their sockets, and his features showed that he was in pain, from some inward hell, which seemed to set his brain on

94

fire. After recovering her self-composure and strength, Paula approached his bedside, and laid her hand on her father's hot and forehead.

A long, loud scream rang out on from his lips, and a piercing cry, "It is she! Yes, it is she! I see, I see! Ah! No, this is not my daughter! She wouldn't come to me if she could!" he shouted.

"I'm your daughter," said Paula. Cleaning his face with her handkerchief, and sobbing.

Like balls of fire, her father's eyes glared up at her, and large drops of perspiration flowed down his pale, emaciated face. Strange as it was, it was a meeting between a father and his long-lost daughter. Kato now ordered all present to leave the room, except the nurse, and every effort was made to save the dieing man. A calm and joyous smiles showed on Kenneth's face, and a teary light beamed in his eyes, as he seemed to realize that elegant woman that stood before him was his daughter.

For seven long days and nights Paula sat at the bedside of her father before he could speak to her intelligently. Sometimes, in his insane fits, he would talk wildly in frightful manners, and then, in a few moments, would go back to his old ways, often acting childish. At last, after a long and refreshing sleep, he recovered and realized that it was his daughter who was taking care of him, and, patiently waiting by his side.

The presence of his daughter had a soothing effect upon Kenneth, and he was recovering rapidly from the sad hopeless condition in which she had found him. When able to talk, without danger of a relapse, he told Paula of his fruitless efforts to find her after Mrs. Cavalla had sold her to the slave-trader.

"I blamed my wife for your being sold and sent away, I thought she and her mother had worked against me; But afterwards I found out that I had accused her wrongfully. Poor woman! She knew I loved your mother. My wife died three years ago."

Paula and her father wept at the thought of those days. When they recovered their composure, Mr. Oar continued: "Mrs. Cavalla," he said, "after the death of Loretta, aware that she had contributed much toward her unhappiness, started drinking, and became the most brutal creature that ever lived.

She whipped her slaves without reason, and seemed to take delight in inventing new ways with which to punish them. One night last winter, after having flogged one of her slaves nearly to death, she returned to her room, she was drunk, falling down nasty dirty stinking, drunk. By some unknown means her bedding was on fire. Her bedroom was in flames before any one was awake. There was no one in the mansion at the time but the old woman and one slave. The latter might have fallen on her mistress. None of helped her. After mistreating her slaves for many years, she died a most miserable death, without a single friend."

Paula wiped the tears from her eyes, as her father finished this story, although Mrs. Cavalla had been her greatest enemy, she regretted to learn that her death had been such a sad and brutal one.

"My peace of mind was destroyed after you left," continued her father, "and my health got worst, my physician advised me to travel, with the hope of recovering, I sailed from Boston two months ago."

Every day Mr. Oar became more and more familiar with Kato, and eventually they were on the most intimate terms. Thirty days from the time that Paula was taken to her father's room, she left the hotel with her husband and father. Aware that her father was still a slave-owner, Paula used all of her influence to get him to set them free.

Liberty Dendron

"I have always treated my slaves well," said Mr. Oar to Kato, as the he expressed his hatred of the system; "and my neighbors, too, are good men, slavery in Virginia is not like slavery in some parts of the south," I'm still a proud son of the Old Dominion.

It was with pleasure that Paula got from her father a promise that he would free all his slaves when he returned to Cape Charles. In a village sourounded by deep blue lake, Mr. Oar, Paula, and Kato, lived in a rented country home for a short time. For more than three weeks, the three of them spent their time hunting, fishing, and reading. After a stay of four weeks in Italy, Mr. Oar set out for America, with the full determination of freeing his slaves, and settling them in one of the Northern States, and return to Italy to the remainder of his life with his daughter.

When the first guns were fired at the American Flag, on the 12th of April, 186; at Fort Sumter. Those shots reverberated all over Europe, the downfall of American slavery had begun. Most citizens, of the United States, visiting abroad, rushed home to take part in the Civil War. Some to side of the rebels, others to take their stand with the friends of liberty. Among the retuning slaves, none came with swifter steps or more passion than Kato and Paula Amid. They arrived in South Carolina a week after the capture of the city.

The city had changed very little since Paula had last set feet on South Carolina soil! Twenty-two years had passed, her life had changed many times sincene then, her old friends in South Carolina had disappeared. With the exception of the black faces which she saw at every turn, and which in her younger days were her friends, she felt as if she were in the midst of strangers. Whites and blacks were fighting each other in mortal combat. With ample means, Mr. and Mrs. Fletcher started helping injured and sick slaves. With a heart overflowing with human kindness, and a tear for every sufferer, Paula was called the Angel of Mercy.

The order issued on the 22nd of August, 1862, recognize ing, and calling into the service of the Federal Government, the battalion of colored men known as the African Platoon, at once gave full scope to Kato's military enthusiasm; he quickly joined it. There was a bloody battle when they entered Greenville near the end of the day, the attack on Greenville proved the undying spirit and bravery of black soldiers, and the undying hate and bravery of rebel soldiers. The field was scattered with dead. The dying. Wounded, and as the worn-out regiments were leaving the ground, after their unsuccessful attack, it was found that Capt. Westbrook, of the Third South Carolina, had been killed; and his body, which was easily seen because of his uniform. He was lying on the battle-field.

The colonel of the regiment, asked. "Are there four men here who will fetch the body of Capt. Westbrook from the field?" Four men stepped up, and were slaudered like cattle by the confederate army. They hit them with everything they had, riffles firing and cannons blasting. The question was again repeated, "Are there men who will go for the body?" Nine black men had been killed trying to retrieve one white dead officer. "Is there anyone that will go and get Capt. Westbrook?" shouted the officer. Four men stepped forward, one was Kato. They started running and all of them reached the body, and had nearly returned to their line, when two of the men were shot down. One was Kato. His head was torn off by a cannon shell, but the body of the officer was retrieved.

CHAPTER 12

THE WAR

The news of Kato's death was brought to Paula while she was helping the sick and wounded that filled the hospitals. For hours she hid from staring eyes. Few marriages had been happier than theirs, this blow, so unexpected, nearly destroyed her. Reading newspapers describing suffering of slave and Union prisoners throughout the south mad her angry. The pain was too great, she left South Carolina.

It was the month of October, when Paula arrived in Savannah. She entered the rebel camps to carry out her plans. She lived with a private family, and continued her work. She first visited the hospitals, tents of which were horrible excuses for hospitals. It was the beginning of November, even in the Deep South it was so cold your fingers and toes got numb: nights and mornings were extremely cold. Soulders lay in dirty, unventilated tents. Straw and leaves was thrown on the ground for beds. The beds, upon which lay the ragged, starving sick Union prisoners. Most suffering with diseases bought on from starvation. Seeing the suffering, and cruelty these men had endured; made her sad.

Having volunteered to work in hospitals in Europe, and amongst the sick at South Carolina. Paula's knew sending a little money, would make the prisoners comfortable. The hate of Union prisoners was so apparent, she was determined to do what she could, she worked season after season.

The brutal treatment and daily murders of union soldiers in Savannah prisons caused Paula to secretly help prisoners to escape. In the latter work, she brought with her an assistant a slave named

99

Poky. He cleaned the prison, and, having the entire confidence of the confederate officers, he was in a position to do things without being suspected. Poky had a cheerful nature, and, but when planning an escape, he was very serious, and usually sang a sad song. For several weeks, the prisoners worked at night digging a tunnel. All but the digging upward outside of the prison wall was done. The digging was a slow dirty project. The prisoners had to dig atleast ten feet below the earth. After digging and covering the floor, they dug nearly fifty feet to get beyond the wall. The digging was done.

The day arrived. The prisoners prepared to leave the prison by the tunnel. They waited for the signal. The time came. The hole was uncovered, and the first man entered the tunnel and crawled to the end and had barely put his head out of the hole, when he was fired upon by one of the guards, who sounded the soon alarmed and the entire guard rushed to the spot. The word of the attempt to escape rushed throughout the prison, and those were trapped in the tunnel were severely punished.

A heavy iron was placed on legs and arms the prisoners, and their stay was made even harder by the guards. Paula was allowed to see the prisoners; she took care of their wants, and, knew nothing of the intended escape. The cruelty which followed this mishap, inspired Paula to help then in another escape, but the men were heavily ironed. Poky, whose sympathies was with the Union prisoners, was easily influenced to help, he promise of get the keys to the prison chains and unlock the door too let the men escape; when Paula of-fered him money so that he could escape to the North.

The night of the mass departure came. It was favored with darkness, and it so happened that the officials were busy, preparing for the arrival of high ranking Confederate officers. Before getting the keys, Poky took the guards on duty enough whiskey to make them drunk, which he had stolen from the store-room. At the chosen moment, the keys were taken by Poky, the doors and gates were opened, and the prisoners, including ones in irons escaped, taking Poky with them. Nothing was known of the excape untill the next morning. On examination of the store-room, it was found, that, in addition to the whiskey Poky took a great deal of food for the escaping prisoners. Added to this, a wagon of rifles and ammunition had been given to the prisoners by Poky.

The confederate soldiers were not prepared to successfully pursue the fleeing prisoners, the prisoners had scattered in different directions.   Nothin was heard of them till they had reached the Union lines. Long suspected of aiding Union prisoners, Paula was charged with having knowledge of the escape; she was forced to leave Savannah. Another woman was arrested while on a visit to Greenville with medicine and other necessaries for sick Yankee soldiers captured by confederate soldiers. She had her horse taken from her, and robbed of the things she had purchased. After experiencing near death at the hands of the southern women. She was released, penniless, without the means of reaching her home in Maryland; when Paula, who had just arrived at the hotel, met her. Learning what had happened, she offered to help Carole, which brought down upon her the raft of white people.

Paula purchased a horse from the landlord and gave it to Carol who, left town after dark. The people in Greenville were angry with her because she helped Carole escape. Paula's trunks and letters were searched with hope of finding evidence that she was of a spy, but nothing was found. She was then interrogated. They asked her questions about the two warring armies. With no wish now to conceal her thoughts any longer, she told them she was a Yankee sympathizer. This was enough. After being mistreated during the day, she was guarded by a slave woman that night; with a promise of more violent treatment the following day. One of the servants overheard the rebels in a conversation, they were going to send Paula to another town, to another jail, the following day; this was told to Paula. The servant told Paula, "I'll help you escape."

The clock in the narrow hall way struck one. Rain was pounding on the roof, the women guards one after another, had fallen asleep; a tenseness and nervousness had fallen over the room and kept them awake longer than was expected, when Harriett, a servant entered the room gesturing to Paula, they left in silence. Cautiously and softly Harriett led the way, followed by Paula, passing down through the cellar with water covering the floor, they came out in the back yard. Two horses had been provided. Paula mounted one and a black man the other; the man leading the way. They dashed off at a rapid pace, through a drenching storm; it was so darkthey could barely see each other.

After an hour's ride the man stopped, and told Paula that he must leave, and return with the horses. He said you're with friends! He whistled... for a moment he held his breath. He was about to signal again, but he heard the response; and seconds later a lady stepped out of the darkness, with dripping garments, Paula followed her guide to a cabin in the woods.

"You're as wet as I am," said the woman, who met Paula as she entered the cabin.

"Yes," replied Paula, "a stormy night to be out in."

"Yes mam, these are hard times for everybody that 'believes in freedom for slaves. They caught your husband, and put him in the army, didn't they?"

"No: my husband died at Greenville, fighting confederate soldiers," said Paula.

"Oh, mam, that's the where black people, fought the rebels, wasn't it?" Remarked Ella.

"Yes, that was the place," replied Paula. "I noticed that your man has lost one of his hands, did he lose it in the war?"

When they was taken men, black and white, to put in the army, they caught my man, and took him with 'em. He said he'd die before he'd shoot at the Yankee soldier. So you see, miss, Wesley placed his left hand on a log, and chop it off with the hatchet. And they let him go, and he came home. You see, miss, my Wesley is a free man: he was born free, and he bought me, he payid five hundred dollars for me."

After a week hiding in this cabin, Jim took Paula through the Yankee lines, and from there she went to Wilmington North Carolina.

The Rebellion was now drawing to a close. The towns and cities on the Atlantic had been taken by the Yankees. Sherman was on his raid, and Grant was raining in Lee. Everywhere the condition of the freedmen attracted the attention of the friends from the north, and no one was happier than Paula; she decided to devote the remainder of her life, and for this purpose went to the State of Virginia, and opened a school; hired teachers, paying them out of her own pocket. The summer of 1868, Paula Vaga bought the plantation, she was born. She never returned to Italy or saw her son again.

www.ingramcontent.com/pod-product-compliance
Lightning Source LLC
Chambersburg PA
CBHW030339020726
47493CB00004B/1335